These Daisies Told
The Casebook of
Professor Ulysses Price Middlebie

Other book collections by Arthur Porges:

Three Porges Parodies and a Pastiche (1988)
The Mirror and Other Strange Reflections (2002)
Eight Problems in Space: The Ensign De Ruyter Stories (2008)
The Adventures of Stately Homes and Sherman Horn (2008)
The Calabash of Coral Island and Other Early Stories (2008)
The Miracle of the Bread and Other Stories (2008)
Spring, 1836: Selected Poems (2008)
The Devil and Simon Flagg and Other Fantastic Tales (2009)
The Curious Cases of Cyriack Skinner Grey (2009)
The Ruum and Other Science Fiction Stories (2010)
The Rescuer and Other Science Fiction Stories (2014)
Unusual Plants of the Galaxy (2014)
No Killer Has Wings: The Casebook of Dr. Joel Hoffman (2017)

Forthcoming titles by Arthur Porges:

The Price of a Princess: Hardboiled Crime Fiction
Collected Essays: Volume One
Collected Essays: Volume Two

Books by F. W. Thomas (from the same publisher):

Tales From Stonecutter Street (2010)
Star Turns (2011)
The Rising Sap (2013)

Books by Basil Wells (from the same publisher):

Final Voyage and Other Science Fiction Stories (2016)

These Daisies Told
The Casebook of
Professor Ulysses Price Middlebie

Arthur Porges

Edited by Richard Simms

Richard Simms Publications

Contents

Introduction

In recent years I have collected in book form those "impossible crime" stories by Arthur Porges featuring the sleuths Cyriack Skinner Grey and Dr. Joel Hoffman. Given the interest in these volumes among fans of the author's output in this area of mystery fiction, it occurred to me that I was guilty of a major discrepancy in not assembling together the crime-puzzle stories that comprise the series starring Professor Ulysses Price Middlebie.

An armchair criminologist, recently retired as Professor (Emeritus) of the History and Philosophy of Science, Middlebie is called upon by his friend and erstwhile pupil, Detective Sergeant Black, to help investigate a variety of perplexing crimes in the eleven stories that make up this collection.

The crimes themselves, as was typical for Porges, are unusual in method: these are not *whodunits* but *howdunits*. Utilizing Middlebie's wide-ranging knowledge, and his imaginative ability to "think outside the box," in each of these tales, the sergeant, after he and his police colleagues have investigated and ruled out all the obvious solutions, presents the professor with a problem to solve. At times it is the challenge of working out an ingenious murder method, or an enigma surrounding how a theft was performed—despite seemingly airtight security measures. At others, the mystery involves a way of carrying out arson while leaving no trace of the means used, or a race against time to ascertain the modus operandi and prevent a murder from happening. Whatever the gimmick, I trust connoisseurs of Porges' work in this sub-genre will find much to admire here.

If the above set-up sounds familiar, it is, of course, the tried and tested formula of the brilliant criminologist helping out a police detective stumped by a seemingly unsolvable case. This is a story framework the author used time and again in his crime fiction, and was largely inspired by the Sherlock Holmes stories of Sir Arthur Conan Doyle. Indeed, Holmes, along with his elder brother Mycroft, is referenced several times by Middlebie in more than one story.

Most of the Middlebie stories were published in *Alfred Hitchcock's Mystery Magazine* during the early 1960s. Another was sold to *Mike Shayne Mystery Magazine*, while "Small, Round Man From Texas" (1964) was first printed in *This Week*, a Sunday supplement magazine to several U.S. newspapers which included *The Los Angeles Times*. Bibliographers may be curious to know it reappeared later the same year in *The Australian Women's Weekly*. Of course, for short stories to be syndicated internationally in this way was common practice. But given this story's original publication history, it is something of a rarity, and will have been missed by the majority of those who subscribed to the regular crime fiction digests. Because of this I am especially pleased to present it here. One final Middlebie tale, "Fire for Peace," appeared in the May 1975 issue of *Ed McBain's 87th Precinct Mystery Magazine*. It is a shame the series came to an abrupt halt there.

Those interested in background may be intrigued to learn the partial inspiration behind the name of this particular sleuth. Arthur had many heroes within the field of science, and Middlebie is so named in honor of the Scottish mathematical physicist James Clerk Maxwell (1831-1879), whose ancestry goes back to the Middlebie estate in Scotland.

Another nice personal touch by Porges can be found in the various references to local bird life. Middlebie is a keen ornithologist, at times more excited at spotting a rare bird than solving a homicide! Inspired by his friend Francis Raymond, Arthur himself became very interested in birdwatching, and was able to identify many different species in Southern California, the region where this series is set. I like the way he brings his passion for the subject into these stories.

It is difficult for me to choose a personal favorite among the tales gathered here. Certainly "Coffee Break" (1964) is an acknowledged classic in the field, a real bona fide "locked room" mystery, this one! It has been reprinted several times before, but at the time of writing, not for almost thirty years. "The Missing Bow" (1963) is not only clever but has real emotive power with its theme of retribution. However, the one I am most fond of is probably the title story, "These Daisies Told" (1962), a masterpiece of invention, great dialogue and concise writing. As always, I was completely unable to guess the solution (in this case the hidden location of a murdered wife's body), but other readers may have more luck. Looking back through my correspondence with Arthur, I found he thought this was one of his cleverest ideas and rated the story quite highly.

Well, I have gone on long enough. Have fun discovering your own favorites in this collection, and enjoy the ride with the estimable Professor Ulysses Price Middlebie. Though I would not recommend sharing his preferred tipple of bourbon, beer and brown sugar!

Richard Simms
Surrey, England
May, 2018

These Daisies Told

Not many men can begin a new and fascinating career at the age of sixty-five. But Ulysses Price Middlebie, Professor (Emeritus) of the History and Philosophy of Science, was one of the few, and this is an account of his first case.

Unlike most of his senior colleagues at Bateman University, he saw no reason to kick and scream over the loss of a captive audience. Although he enjoyed teaching, Middlebie had other resources. For he was a man with an enormous zest for living. Not just the life of the intellect, although that was probably his favorite mode of existence; but also the life of blood-and-bone. To him, retirement was merely a welcome change from the classroom to the open fields and busy tide-pools.

He was a tall, lean man, big-boned, and with the springy step of a boy. His physical fitness was due, undoubtedly, to many years of the "endless quest," as he called the search for knowledge. As President of the local Audubon Society, he made the study of birds only one phase in his development as a well-rounded naturalist. Middlebie could identify over two hundred species of birds in Southern California, often from just a glance at their flights or wing-patterns. He was equally at home with plants and hundreds of small animals, including, naturally, insects; the common sea-shells; and even the constellations overhead. With his brisk sparrow of a wife he had studied flora and fauna from San Diego to Santa Barbara. In short, he had the background to be expected—but not often found—in a man who presumed to teach the History and Philosophy of Science.

It was because of this universal grasp of nature that the professor acquired his niche as consultant in crime. He was used to teaching new members of the Audubon Society the difference between a plover and a sandpiper; just as he was ready to explain that the striped, fearsome-looking "bug" in a neighbor's garden was merely a harmless sluggish Jerusalem cricket. But it had never occurred to him that he was uniquely qualified to catch criminals.

If Detective Sergeant Black hadn't been one of Middlebie's students, the contact, which later proved so valuable to the police, might never have been made. But the officer remembered how quickly, on field trips, the old man's unerring eyes had found and interpreted correctly, all those little indicators that speak volumes to a naturalist. That memory inspired him to ask for the professor's help in a time of trial, when his own career as a detective hung in the balance.

He outlined his difficulties as they sat in Middlebie's study, a large, sunny room, crammed with books and fragrant with the odor of good tobacco.

"It's the matter of a missing body," Black told him. "Without it, we don't have much of a case, but we're certain the woman is dead—murdered."

"Perhaps you'd better give me all the available facts," the professor said mildly. If he was surprised at the type of problem presented to a retired teacher, he didn't show it. A missing body, philosophically speaking, was no different from any other object absent from its normal place in the universe. And nothing could be altered in the real world without affecting other objects around it. Given enough of such changes, and the sequence of events could be reconstructed.

"There isn't very much to tell," the sergeant said. Then he added hastily: "I know, sir, you always stressed the fact that we must note everything possible relating to a scientific problem; even if some of the information seems to have no connection at the time."

"That's quite right. Nobody is ever in a position to know right at the start which data are relevant. And they might not be available later if missed at the beginning. In the case of Faraday and his discovery of induction—but I mustn't digress—that's one sin of old age I mean to fight. Go ahead, Sergeant."

"Well, to put it bluntly, we're practically sure that this man, Dale Corsi, has killed his wife; but we can't find her body."

Middlebie's eyebrows rose slightly, and Black winced. He knew the mannerism. He had noted it in class when somebody had formed a unique specific conclusion from facts which warranted only several, alternate explanations.

"I'd like to hear your reasons," the professor said.

"It's simple, in a way. She's been gone for a week—disappeared completely; and nobody has seen her around or even heard from her."

"But this is a heavily populated area. One person could easily vanish if she chose to."

"Not in this case, I think you'll agree. They live on a small ranch, quite off the main highway. She didn't take her car, and there are very few buses going by that would stop there. We found no record of anybody matching her description who left the area by any reasonable means."

"That's still not mathematical proof; although I'm sure you know that. But what does her husband—Corsi, you said?—say?"

"He maintains she must have left him; that they hadn't been getting along. The last part is true enough. We found some bloodstains in the house, but unfortunately he and his wife have the same type. So when he showed us a cut on his arm, our evidence was pretty useless. It's a million to one he cut himself purposely to account for his wife's blood, but we can't prove that either."

"Ingenious fellow," Middlebie said dryly. "Any motive?"

"Plenty. As I said, they hated each other. In addition, she owned the ranch and brought scads of money to the marriage. The cash is in a joint account—or was—he drew it out almost immediately, and deposited it in a new account, under his own name, individually."

"That would be to keep the state from tying it up once her disappearance was known."

"Right. We're told she was ready to knock his name off anyhow. That's one more reason for him to kill her."

"On the other hand, until she's presumed dead, which could take years if you don't find the body, he couldn't do much about her other assets."

"That's true; but we don't contend the murder was carefully planned in cold blood. He may have lost his temper. But afterwards he managed to get rid of—or destroy—the body; that's what has us stumped."

"I'm not clear why that should puzzle you. There are thousands of acres of farmland where a body could be buried."

"Not in this case." The sergeant spoke with conviction. "Corsi himself doesn't drive. There's a high fence around the ranch that would take some doing to get a body over or through. The neighboring places are all heavily cultivated just now—beans, orange groves, walnut trees; stuff like that. The sort of terrain where any grave would be found the next day. No, we figure the body has to be on his own land, unless it's been totally destroyed, which is not only unlikely, but is damned near impossible."

"All right, then; what makes you certain it's not on the Corsi property?"

"All I know is that we can't find it," Black said in a bitter voice. "The ground cover, mostly ice-plant, hasn't been disturbed. Neither have the flower beds his wife planted, although one looked mighty suspicious at first. We even used bloodhounds to trace Corsi's movements; but they just proved he didn't leave the ranch recently. Naturally, his tracks were found all over the place; he walks quite a lot."

"You say he's an artist. How good?"

"Not very—at least, that's what the critics tell us. One of them explained he has some talent, but dabbles too much, and wastes it. He paints in both oils and watercolors, sculpts a little; uses any old material around: wood, concrete—even those crazy things made from rusty junk. 'Spirit of a Dead Hot Rod,' one of them is called. It's in the house—ugh! What the hell do people see in stuff like that?"

The professor chuckled.

"I wouldn't know; I'm rather a conservative about art and music. But I'm not foolish enough to condemn it en masse without knowing more about the subject. However, Corsi's versatility could be significant. He has a loose and active imagination, apparently. Maybe he made good use of it to dispose of the body. If there is one," he added, with a sly twinkle in his wide-set grey eyes.

"You bet there's one," was the sergeant's grim retort. "With our own routines we're very efficient. If that woman had left the grounds, we'd have had some evidence to that effect. There's always somebody who sees something; believe me, I know."

"But you say the place is rather isolated."

"True; but she wouldn't go across country. Not a frail little thing—which is what she was. You know how those fields are. She'd have to go several hundred yards down a dirt road to the highway, and then either wait for a bus, or hitch a ride. But all her clothes are still in the house. No, Professor, he got rid of her body somehow. After all, he had almost a week before she was missed."

"Let me summarize the situation before I look for solutions. You've examined every foot of the ranch, and found no grave."

"That's right. We didn't miss any of it. There are only a few acres, and I used a dozen good men who know what to look for."

"And I presume there's no evidence of dissection, burning, or acids—not that they'd be feasible, actually. The human body is very hard to destroy completely."

"Almost impossible."

Professor Middlebie stood up.

"It's time I had a look, then. The armchair phase seems to be over. Now I need data at first hand. Assuming you're right, and the body is actually hidden on the ranch, we should be able to find it."

"I sure hope so," the sergeant said fervently. "The captain is riding my back like a jockey." They left.

"A nice place," Middlebie said, as they explored the small ranch. "Suffering from drought like all this region, but basically good. Notice the huge rocks that crop out here and there almost as if deliberately planned for scenic effect. They're granite; magnificent things. And I see somebody planted zinnias near this one."

"If you're thinking she's under one of the rocks," Sergeant Black said, "I'd forget that angle. There are only about three small enough to be moved even with a heavy tow-truck. He doesn't drive, remember, and the only car on the ranch is a little station wagon, anyhow. But we looked those three smaller rocks over very carefully. They haven't been budged."

"I know that," Middlebie said, a bit tartly. "It would be impossible to move them without disturbing soil and vegetation, even if the tools were available." He looked up as a flock of birds sailed by. "Curlews. Flying to the Bay." He studied the granite mass for a moment, and said: "If this was sandstone, a man might even make a hollow in it big enough for a body, given a few days to work. But not in granite—trained sculptor or John Henry himself." He peered at the patch of zinnias, and a faint frown touched his mobile face. His grey eyes were suddenly cloudy with thought.

"Look at those plants at the edge of the flower bed," he told Black. "Notice how spindly they are? Taller than the rest, but thin and scraggly. Even their colors are not as bright."

There was a harsh, cawing sound in the distance; the old man smiled.

"Raven," he said. "Fascinating pirate of a bird."

"We didn't miss these flowers," the sergeant said. "They're the one suspicious spot I mentioned at your house. But it's a false lead. We probed with rods, far down, and it's certain the ground hasn't been dug into. In fact, if you look closely, it's clear the soil hasn't been touched for months."

"Oh, I agree," Middlebie said. "Of course, there's no body under these zinnias. But everything in nature has a cause. I ask you, Sergeant, why this one part of a flower bed should be so atypical?"

"I don't know," Black replied, a little impatiently. The old boy was a bit pompous and longwinded today. Maybe he'd lost whatever had impressed the pupil of five years back. "Poorer soil there, maybe; disease; I'm no botanist. What's your theory?"

"I don't have one yet. Remember—first comes the harvest of the eye. Then the crop must be winnowed, to separate the wheat from the chaff. My eye has noted these aberrant flowers; what that fact means, if anything, in relation to our problem, is not clear. But I'll be winnowing mentally as we finish our inspection of the ranch. After you, Sergeant."

Black started to move away, but the old man stood there listening. A faint snapping sound came from a tree.

"Audubon warbler," the professor announced, to nobody in particular. Then he followed the detective.

An hour later, they returned to the same spot. Middlebie had seemed alert enough, but Black felt that one part of the old man's mind was still busy with the zinnias.

"Well?" he asked the professor, as they stood near the large granite rock overshadowing the red and yellow blossoms.

"I'm inclined to agree with you that there's no grave on this ranch. If you're convinced he had no means to destroy the remains physically—"

"I'm convinced."

"Then it's hidden some other way. Purloined letter style, perhaps."

"But where, damn it? You've been over the place. Is this guy going to get away with it clean, just because he found some cute way of hiding a hundred pounds of flesh-and-blood right under our noses?"

"I'd like to get up on the rock for a minute," the professor said quietly.

Black gaped at him.

"There's nothing up there. The top's in plain sight. Oh," he added, looking sheepish. "You want to make a survey of the place from a higher point."

"No," Middlebie said. "That's not the idea at all." He moved to one side of the rock. "This is a good spot, right here. How about a boost? Just link your hands—come on, man." Bewildered, the detective did as he was told. With a litheness uncommon in a person his age, the professor put one foot in the sergeant's hands, and by clutching the edge of the huge boulder, pulled himself smoothly to the rugged, tilted surface. He got to his feet, then stooped to scrutinize the granite top. Rising, he repeated his inspection at two other places. Finally he stood on the very edge, peering down at Black.

"The zinnia is a flower that thrives on sunlight, and suffers badly without it," he said, as if addressing a class. "If you suddenly cut off a good part of the summer sunshine, the plant soon becomes spindly; it grows faster and higher trying to make up the loss—reaching for the light, you might say, just as we have been today.

"Now, why should one part of a flower bed abruptly be short of light? It's an interesting question. Certainly the sun's rays are not discriminating. The only reason I could think of was new shade. From somewhere, caused by something, a shadow fell upon these few plants—a shadow that wasn't there a week ago. It couldn't have been caused by the season; not with longer days still to come. What's the answer?" He scrambled down without asking for help, and stood beside the sergeant, looking up at the massive rock.

"What do you see on top?" the professor asked him. "Take a good look."

"Not a damned thing," Black replied, circling the boulder. "Just a rough surface of rock full of ridges and humps. I don't know what you're getting at."

"A very competent artist, Corsi," Middlebie said. "It's no wonder you don't spot his work up there. He molded a mausoleum on top of the rock, using concrete and coloring with wonderful expertise. Even from my position right alongside, I had to take a very careful look to be sure. His concrete mix has the texture and hue of the granite; in addition, he even shaped the mass to continue the proper contours for that part of the rock. After all, who would notice a relatively small increase in the total bulk—a mound roughly the size of a little woman, and blended with the many tons around it? Just a tiny change in the dimensions. Most people see without really comprehending, anyway. I suppose few of them ever gave this magnificent outcropping more than a passing glance.

"Yes, Sergeant, she's up there, all right, along the left edge. It's a pity," he added in a lower voice, "that she can't be left just where we found her. To be on top of a sunny rock, with the birds flying near, overlooking orchards and green fields, surely that's better than a hole in the ground." He was silent for a moment, his face grave. Then he brightened a little, and gestured towards the patch of glowing flowers.

"Do you know, Sergeant, zinnias are members of the daisy family—but these finally did tell."

The Unguarded Path

Ulysses Price Middlebie, formerly Professor of the History and Philosophy of Science, had begun a new career at the age of sixty-five. Actually it was almost the old one all over again, in a different frame of reference.

Where before he had taught—from the sources—the principles of scientific investigation, working his way down (or up) from Archimedes to Salk, Middlebie now practiced what he had preached: that is, he applied his comprehensive knowledge of logic to the solutions of problems in crime.

A man who can identify hundreds of birds on the wing, tell one obscure mineral formation from another, enlarge on the odd reproductive habits of the plant louse, or solve a matrix equation, might seem more a freak of nature than a practical detective. But that idea happens to be quite fallacious. It takes sound theory to support good field work; and the professor, if his head was in the clouds, had feet that gripped the earth like the hoofs of a mountain goat.

The books are very clear about the difference between Cassin's kingbird and the Western species, but it takes a quick eye to spot the almost invisible fringe of white along the bottom of the tail—the field mark that settles the matter. And Middlebie's cavernous grey eyes had seldom been known to misread any of nature's signs.

His one-time pupil, Detective Sergeant Black, had been the first person to utilize the professor's unique talents. Thanks to Middlebie, Black had broken one puzzling case, involving the disappearance of a body. Now the young detective was back. A sensible fellow, devoid of false pride, he was happy to accept competent help where he knew it could be found.

"They're out to kill Franklin Devoe," Black explained in his deep, slow voice. "He was the lawyer for the Syndicate. Now he's going to talk, and they have to shut him up. Devoe knows where all the bodies are buried, and his ex-employers are desperate."

Middlebie eyed him from under shaggy brows that suggested plumage. They were in the old man's study, a large room consisting chiefly of books, all neatly ordered on floor to ceiling shelves. The professor was tall, lean, and big-boned, with the vigor of a boy, maintained, no doubt, by frequent hikes across rough country in search of assorted specimens.

Like a well known Justice of the Supreme Court, he was fully capable of outwalking the whole of Congress, from the smallest pageboy to the oldest senator. On the other hand, he was too tactful and kindly a man to humiliate anybody, and often stopped for a breather, which he no more needed than an antelope would after trotting fifty feet on an open plain.

"I'm not sure just what you expect of me this time," Middlebie said. "No crime has been committed. Surely you have the man under guard."

"That's right—we do," Black replied. "He's staying in his house—an estate, actually, and we have him covered the way they watched Khrushchev when he came to New York two years ago."

Middlebie cocked his head. "So?"

"Ordinarily I wouldn't be worried, because the place is crawling with our men—good ones. They patrol the grounds and stay right with Devoe, night and day. We watch his wife and two kids just as carefully."

"Then what is the problem, precisely?"

"The letters mostly. They're getting under my skin."

The deep-set grey eyes narrowed slightly. "Letters? Perhaps you'd better explain!"

"It's like this. The Syndicate must have sent East for their best killer. We've heard about this guy, but he's never been booked or fingerprinted. Nobody can tell us what he looks like, and even if we spotted him, there's no charge that would stand up in court. Without meaning any disrespect, sir, he's almost a kind of criminal Professor Middlebie!

"They call him the 'Genius.' His real name is Joe Vasta, although I wouldn't bet on the authenticity of that, either. Anyhow, he knows a lot about science and literature. He's just not an ordinary hood at all. He's knocked off several guys in ways that left the police flatfooted. Tricks no cop could figure in time. This guy's out of our class, so far."

Middlebie was looking oddly cheerful. Then, realizing that Black was worried, his expression became more sympathetic. What might be an intellectual challenge to him was, quite obviously, a matter of job, prestige, and—to be fair—crime prevention to the sergeant.

"Tell me about those letters," he said.

"Well, Vasta usually sends a whole series of letters to the man he's after. I'm not clear whether he does that to make him nervous and easier to kill, or just for kicks—thumbing his nose at the police, so to speak. Maybe both. In our case, he's bothering us in several ways.

"First of all, he knows all about our precautions. That's not too surprising, though. The Syndicate has millions, and there's always one or two cops on any force who will take bribes. If I knew this one," Black gritted, "I'd skin him alive. But all I mean is, that part isn't any great puzzle."

"Then what is?"

"This. He practically tells us what he's up to, and yet we remain in the dark about his exact plans. Devoe is supposed to testify before the Grand Jury on Wednesday. Vasta writes that he means to do the job Tuesday night. He says that Devoe will be dead by midnight, and adds that he may send some of the family and a few lousy cops with him. Funny part is, he urges us to take the wife and kids away; apparently he doesn't want to hurt them. Yet it may be a trick to reach Devoe through them."

"That suggests something like a bomb, or fire, that doesn't select its victims."

"Right. Only there's no chance of his making use of either. Nothing gets in without a complete check. We even use a portable x-ray machine."

"Where do you get food?"

"From a different supermarket each day, and always from the big assortment of stuff on the shelves. No chance to tamper in advance."

"Tell me about the physical set-up—the house and grounds."

"Actually it should be a cinch to guard. It was made like a fortress. A five-acre estate, well out of the city, with a cyclone fence topped by barbed wire. Plenty of floodlights, and their own gas generator to keep the place lit up in case of a power failure.

"The house has only two outside doors and we have a couple of men on each, with sawed off shotguns. Six men patrol the grounds inside the fence. They have dogs, German shepherds that can smell a stranger before he gets close."

"Sounds pretty thorough," Middlebie said. "The bomb idea can't work in such circumstances. Fire wouldn't necessarily kill anybody—not with so many people alert. Of course," he added wryly, "the killer might set up a fieldpiece or rocket launcher outside the fence."

"Even that wouldn't work," Black said, with a tight grin. "There are three men in a cruiser driving the roads outside the fence. I hardly think anybody could pull a howitzer up unnoticed! Besides, you should see that house. A grenade wouldn't do more than chip the bricks. Hell, neither would one shell or two settle anything. We keep Franklin Devoe in a room without an outside wall."

"That doesn't leave many gaps," the professor admitted. "But if we're to go really far out, what about a light plane or helicopter?"

"Pretty unlikely, but not ruled out. We have two men on the roof with those new Army automatic rifles—the kind you can fire with one hand, and chew up the target. Maybe a jet could whiz by, but any ordinary plane would be riddled."

"I have a feeling," Middlebie said thoughtfully, "that the gimmick is much more simple than we suspect."

"I'm with you," Black said. "This Vasta works like that."

"How many letters altogether?"

"One a day since we began to guard Devoe three weeks ago."

"All about the same?"

"Lately. Before that, they were just generally taunting. Then he began to tell us about our precautions. Finally, a week ago, he hinted that Devoe would be killed late at night. Now the last three, say midnight on Tuesday."

Professor Middlebie was pacing the floor of his study, moving with a springy lightness surprising in a man of his age and build.

"Has this Vasta usually performed according to his threats, or are they meant to be misleading?"

"That's what's bugging us. If he says Devoe will get it at midnight on Tuesday, that's when it will happen if we don't outguess Vasta first."

"I wish you'd come to me sooner. Twenty-four hours isn't much time to figure a clever lad like this one."

"You're right," Black admitted ruefully. "But at first I thought he couldn't possibly get past us. Now I'm uneasy. His confidence, his past record, and naming a specific day and time—well, it really gets you down! We need Devoe alive. You don't know how close the Syndicate is coming to taking over in this city."

"Well, suppose you give me a detailed plan of the estate. I'm quite sure you have one. Also a schedule of Devoe's daily routine—if he has one."

"You bet he does—a time for everything. Must be the legal training."

"Any plan of the killer," Middlebie said, "must be related to the layout of the house and grounds, and Devoe's announced timetable."

"I'll have all the stuff here within an hour," Black promised. "It's not for me to coach you, Professor. But the thing is, you must try to get into Vasta's skin, and see in just what way we've left a gap somewhere."

"Your reasoning is good," the old man said dryly. "That's what I had in mind. Possibly it's a purloined letter situation: something so obvious you've missed it. Like the postman in Chesterton's famous story."

"It's not him," Black said, ungrammatically, but with emphasis. "All mail is left at the gate. My men bring it in; then it's carefully screened."

"For what?"

"Packages for bombs, letters for poison or germs."

"Germs aren't too likely," Middlebie said. Then he added more cautiously, "But then, a letter carefully smeared with material from, say, a man with severe infectious hepatitis could knock Franklin Devoe out for a long time—even kill him. Not on schedule, of course, which makes that method improbable. I will say, however, that you're very competent."

Black felt himself flushing with pleasure. Such praise from the professor was not easy to come by, and meant something.

"Thanks," he said. "But if Devoe's dead tomorrow night, I might just as well be no better than the dumbest rookie in Chicken Foot, Arkansas."

Black was glum again as he watched the professor pace the floor.

"We'll hope for a better conclusion," Middlebie said. "Now clear out and let me think about the problem."

Once he was alone, the professor paced the floor for almost an hour, letting his imagination roam freely. When the plans and timetable arrived, he spread them on the huge desk, and made a careful study of all the data.

There was certainly no obvious weakness anywhere inside the fence. That was the first significant clue. Another was the specific time mentioned. Why midnight? Finally, the hint that others might also be killed. That suggested some kind of mass weapon: a shotgun effect.

Then Middlebie concentrated on Devoe's routine. What did the man usually do around midnight? Warm bath at eleven thirty; a moment or two to brush his teeth; then bed. The professor wondered idly about this sequence. Did the average man brush his teeth before or after bathing at bedtime? Quite irrelevant to the problem.

What about the room Devoe was now using as a bedroom? Actually the place was meant for games, but the police had liked its windowless security, and had suggested that Devoe put a bed there. That way, the only entrance was a door guarded by two men, with plenty of others within call. If Vasta planned to kill Devoe in bed at midnight, the professor certainly couldn't see how.

Back to the bathroom. It had a window across from the tub, but Black had scrawled on the blueprint: *Shutters on window must be closed when D inside*. That, plus the men and dogs outside, put the bathroom beyond suspicion. Yet Vasta said midnight, and that's where Devoe would be. It didn't add up.

That left the veiled—well, not so veiled—threat that others might be killed. Bombing was definitely out. So was fire. The only other mass effect Middlebie could think of was wholesale poisoning. But with Detective Sergeant Black's random shopping, and the rigorous inspection of all incoming material—blast it all! What *was* Vasta's angle?

Baffled, the professor took a break. He poured himself an ounce of bourbon, added beer, water from the tap, and a large spoonful of brown sugar. He sipped this weird concoction slowly, but with relish, trying to keep his thoughts from the puzzle. It was a useful technique for escaping a particular rut and allowing the brain to refuel. He stirred the drink idly.

For some reason it was harder than usual to clear his mind, for the problem kept sneaking back. The killer was so confident. Was there a gap in the defenses? Did the most carefully guarded house have secret approaches from the outside?

Then Middlebie stiffened where he sat. There were some classes of things that got in unchecked. Of course! That was it—that had to be it! And so obvious, too.

Excited, he began to retrace Devoe's actions from eleven on. The midnight murder began to make good sense; and the danger to others was also clear, now.

The professor picked up the phone, and called Black. "Sergeant," he said. "Two things. First, how does Devoe bathe? Yes, that's what I said—bathe. Hmm. I see. Two full tubs, one to rinse. I guessed that might be so."

Before hanging up, he asked Black to get one more blueprint. With that, they should be able to trap Vasta at work.

"I'll bring it over myself," the sergeant said, his voice at least two tones above its normal range. "I honestly think you've cracked this one wide open, Professor."

When Black arrived with the blueprint two hours later, furious over the red tape at City Hall, Middlebie showed him, with one lean finger, an unguarded path for murder—one of the three that most houses have.

And so, on Tuesday, just after ten at night, they trapped Joe Vasta himself, well outside the fence, invisible to the patrol car, and with equipment that might have taken many lives inside the house.

"It's worth remembering in the future," the professor said a bit pontifically. "The best guarded house still gets three things more or less unchecked from the outside: Gas, Water, and Electricity. All Vasta had to do was locate the main water line that ran from the big pipe several hundred feet outside the fence into the building. No doubt he went downtown and looked at the same blueprint you secured for me. That's when the idea must have occurred to him.

"Vasta didn't miss a thing. By drawing water for two full tubs, Devoe almost guaranteed a flow from the outside in. If Vasta had finished piercing the pipe, out there in the dark, beyond all patrols, he'd have used that nice little force pump—excellent design there, Black—to shoot a quart or two of poison into the water. When Devoe brushed his teeth and rinsed his mouth—goodbye!

"And anybody else who happened to use tap water about that time would also have died. Notice that he picked a tasteless chemical. It's surprising what a clever man can get even from common garden sprays these days."

"You know," Black said slowly, "with that path to the inside, wouldn't a slender plastic bomb have ended up near the tub? That way, nobody else would get hurt."

"It couldn't get past the valves," Middlebie replied. "Nothing solid could. But," he added rather cryptically, "there are other possibilities with the gas pipes and wiring."

"I'm sure glad you're on our side, Professor!" Black said, but Middlebie wasn't listening to him. His eye was on a large bird, flying past with its long legs trailing.

"Blue heron," the professor said. "Heading for the Bay. You know, I think I'll drive over. They say a reddish egret has come in—almost unheard of around here."

The Missing Bow

"Can a one-armed man with bad legs use a bow-and-arrow to kill somebody? Oddly enough, sir, the answer is yes. He just puts his feet against the inside of the bow, and draws back the string with his good arm. In fact, on some occasions, archers of the past made special long distance flights that way—turning themselves into human crossbows, so to speak."

Professor Ulysses Price Middlebie, once a teacher of the History and Philosophy of Science, and now a sometime crime-consultant, gave Sergeant Black a quizzical stare.

"If that is so, and I'm aware of the truth of your statement, what's the difficulty?"

"That a one-armed man can shoot an arrow very well indeed, if he's practiced a bit, but how does he make the bow vanish into thin air?"

The professor blinked.

"Maybe you'd better explain that."

"I wish I could. All I know is that no bow was found, and that it wasn't possible for him to have disposed of it."

Middlebie was silent for a moment, then he said briskly: "Let's forget the missing bow for a while, and build up some background. I can't work in a vacuum. Who was killed; who's the suspect; and what was the motive, if any?"

"The victim was a Victor Borden—male, white, age thirty-four. I suspect Howard Cole, also white, male, but forty-one years old. As to the motive, that's a cinch. Fifteen months ago, Borden rammed his car into Cole's, killing the man's wife and child—an eight-year-old girl. Cole himself lost his left arm, and was so mangled below the waist that he can just barely hobble around now."

Middlebie looked grim.

"You mean Borden was entirely to blame for the accident?"

"Officially, no. In my opinion, definitely yes. He was going too fast, and had been drinking. Cole had the right-of-way. Borden claimed he acted in time to prevent the crash, but that his brakes failed. Said he'd been having trouble with them for several weeks. His garage mechanic verified that part but insisted he'd fixed them up the day before. But Borden's lawyer—a good man, too good for justice—proved that the mechanic had often been guilty of sloppy work, and even collecting for jobs not done at all. That was enough to confuse the jury. They knew Borden had been drinking and speeding but couldn't be sure about the brakes. What they didn't know—it can't be brought out during the trial—is that Borden has a long record of accidents, reckless driving, suspended licenses, and the rest. He was guilty, all right—to the hilt."

"But got off? Scot-free?"

"No; they gave him a lousy year for involuntary manslaughter. He was out in nine months—about eleven weeks ago, in fact."

"What was his trade, or profession?"

"A small-time fast buck operator, I'd say. Anything to make an easy dollar from some sucker. Not quite illegal, but close. Peddling shoddy merchandise as army surplus—that type of thing."

"And Cole?"

"That's the tragic part. Nominally he manages a sporting goods store. But his real work is as an expert archer. He did all the trick shots for the new 'Robin Hood' shows. Now here he is with one arm and stiff legs. Not to mention his family; he was crazy about them."

"Did he talk about revenge?"

"Not that we can find out. Cole's a reserved, laconic kind of man—a vanishing breed, if you ask me. Still water running deep."

The professor fixed his luminous grey eyes on Black, and said: "He didn't threaten, but you suspect him. Why?"

"Hell, he made it easy—too easy. Listen to this. Cole had a cabby—always the same one—drive him to Borden's flat every night for a week. Between seven and eight each time. He'd leave the cab parked a few feet from the opening to a sort of blind alley. The driver could see him go in, but not what he did towards the end, which was out of sight and dark besides. Let me tell you about that alley. Back doors of stores open into it, and they're all well locked. Nobody leaves his door open in that neighborhood; there are more petty thieves to the block than empty muscatel bottles, and that's saying something.

"Borden lived over a store at the end of the alley. The night of the murder, he was in the bathroom, getting ready to shave; in fact, he was all lathered up, with his back to the open window. A perfect target. The window's about ten feet up, but set back from the store roof so that its distance from the alley where Cole must have stood is nearly thirty feet.

"Well, that night Cole comes in the cab as usual, and hobbles down the alley out of sight. The cabby swears he was carrying only one thing—the thing he always carried in there: a miniature tape-recorder. I'll explain about that later. Anyhow, a few minutes after Cole is out of sight of the cab, the driver hears an awful screech—that's from the woman who lived with Borden—and then Cole comes limping out. Now before he can even get into the cab, a squad car rolls up. It seems that some old lady across the street has noticed the cab pulling in there every night for a week, and the cripple getting out and going into the alley. So that night she can't stand any more, and calls the police."

"I see," Middlebie said thoughtfully. "Cole goes into a blind alley with no bow, comes out the same way, and is captured on the spot."

"That's it," Black moaned. "No chance to hide the bow, even if he smuggled it past the cabby."

"And Borden was killed with an arrow."

"Yes. It had a heavy, sharp point—they tell me it's the kind used for hunting deer and such. It split Borden's spinal cord with one of the sharp edges. He fell, making a crash with junk from the medicine cabinet; that's when his girlfriend screamed."

"You searched the alley, of course."

"You bet. All the doors were locked; there was simply no place to hide even a small bow."

"Was the arrow traced to Cole?"

Black made a grimace.

"He has hundreds of arrows at home—in closets and in the garage. Some are souvenirs of old movies where he did stunt work. How can we identify an arrow from some picture made twenty-five years ago—say Errol Flynn's 'Robin Hood'? It's just a broad-head used for hunting, with only one funny thing about it."

Middlebie seemed to snap to attention.

"What was that?"

"There was a length of string tied to it, an inch or two below the feathers."

"Bow-string?"

"No; just light cord. The archery buffs on the force tell me this stuff could never shoot an arrow; it would break at the first few pounds of pull."

"Then your theory, I take it," Middlebie said slowly, "is Cole, while Borden was in jail, plotted revenge, and learned, possibly, to shoot a bow with one hand. Then he went to Borden's flat when the man was released, and familiarized himself with his habits, learning that Borden was apt to shave or wash between seven and eight. The cab driver was meant to be a witness of sorts—proof that Cole had no bow. The police car merely added to his alibi—a sort of bonus."

"That must be it," Black said, rather glumly. "But with no bow, we don't have a case. It's barely possible he concealed a short one under his jacket, but if so, what happened to it?"

"You searched the roofs, of course."

"Yes; they're accessible only in a couple of places. In all the other ones, the buildings are four to six stories high; nobody could throw a stick up there. But we looked, anyhow. Nothing."

"And a string on the arrow," the professor murmured. "You realize that's the key; it has to be. Anything that doesn't fit is apt to be vital. Like the residue when nitrogen and oxygen were taken from a sample of air. The unexplained discrepancy led to the discovery of the inert gases—now no longer inert at all! Could he have wanted to pull the arrow back after it struck Borden? Why? And that has no connection with the missing bow, anyhow." The grey eyes were turned inward. Then he looked at Sergeant Black again. "Do you have a copy of the medical report?"

"Right here, at your disposal."

"Let me go over that, and do some thinking. I'm sure the data are available to us, and need only the prepared mind for resolution of the problem. Suppose you come back on Wednesday."

"Good," the sergeant said. He knew that once Middlebie put his great store of knowledge and insight to work, there was at least a chance to break this troublesome case. "I'll be back then—unless," he added hopefully, "I hear from you sooner. Tomorrow, say."

"Not very likely," was the dry comment. "Not even Faraday and Pasteur organized experimental data that fast, and I'm at best just playing the ape to their kind."

Black was about to deny this, but said nothing. The professor detested flattery, and often seemed suspicious of honest approval. It was not the worst trait a man could have, the sergeant thought; he knew some people couldn't function without lavish and constant praise. They were the devil to deal with.

So he gave Middlebie a boyish grin, full of warmth more expressive than words, and said: "Good hunting, sir." Then he left.

When Black had gone, the professor sat down at his huge, cluttered desk, and read the medical report. This done, he took pen and paper, and made some rather involved calculations, using a slide-rule from time to time. He studied his results, and his shaggy eyebrows rose. Interesting point, he thought. The arrow had been fired from an unusually weak bow—one of about fifteen pounds pull, his figures indicated—or else the archer had not drawn the string back more than a fraction of its normal range. It was a matter of basic physics. According to the medical report, the heavy, extremely sharp broad-head of steel had just severed the spinal cord. This relatively shallow penetration, when related to the known resistance of tissue, indicated the probable velocity of the arrow, from which the pull of the bow could easily be computed. Naturally it was not an exact determination, but the limits of error were known. Not more than fifteen pounds pull: that was as certain as Newton's Laws themselves.

He wondered then about the length of string: what was its breaking strength? Middlebie looked through some of the other papers in

Black's report. He felt a glow of pleasure at his one-time pupil's competence. The boy had even checked the string. It broke at roughly three pounds of tension. It was obvious the stuff couldn't have functioned as a bow-string.

The professor had a pretty good idea what he ought to do now. He began with the article on archery in the superb 11th Edition of the Encyclopedia, reading it through with great care. He learned much about an ancient and fascinating weapon, but nothing that helped Black's case. Well, tomorrow he'd see what the university library had on archery, just in case. Meanwhile, there was another phase to work on.

He called the nearest sporting goods store, and had them send over a hunting arrow. When it arrived, he examined it closely, and then proceeded to experiment. Using a carefully calibrated spring device he improvised in his own well stocked laboratory, he fired the arrow at a large block of wax which approximated human flesh in density. The experiment verified his calculations; the bow could not have had more than a fifteen-pound pull.

The professor sat there, hefting the arrow in one hand. Suddenly his body tensed with excitement. He stood up, and gripping the center of the shaft, hurled the arrow with all his might at the wax target. It wobbled feebly through the air, struck the very edge of the wax block, then sagged to the floor. He tried several times from a distance of thirty feet, each shot being checked for penetration. He sighed, and put the arrow on the table. Another good idea gone to pot through experimentation. It obviously wasn't possible to throw an arrow hard enough to kill a man at thirty feet. Aside from the problem of aiming it, which would seem to be bad enough, the flight path resembled that of a drunken owl in a high wind. Middlebie dropped the problem for that day. He had less faith than ever in tomorrow's library work, but knew better than to skip it without a trial.

This attitude was fully justified by his session at the university. How odd that a book sixty years old should hold the secret to a recent murder. Yet there it was, in a fat tome called "The Crossbow," just reprinted after more than half a century of neglect. The only trouble was, what should be done now? In theory, the puzzle was solved, but getting a conviction was not so simple. Besides, the professor, although perfectly law abiding, wasn't certain he wanted one.

In the circumstances, he decided to call on the suspect, who was still at home, under surveillance, but not arrest, the police being cautious about the lost bow.

He found Cole to be a thickset, chunky man, whose face, once good humored enough, the professor inferred from the wrinkle-lines of laughter at the corners of the eyes, was now a bitter mask. He walked stiffly, with great deliberation, and seemed charged with restlessness. His right arm, in the thin, short sleeve, was powerfully muscled, as if all the man's strength was now concentrated there.

As Black had said, he was indeed laconic, so that Middlebie had to open the conversation, and carry most of it.

"So you see," he told Cole gently, "the sergeant asked for my help, your ingenuity having baffled him completely, as well it might."

Cole said nothing, but his blue eyes, cold as polar ice, flickered briefly.

"Black thought there was a bow that disappeared, but we know better," the professor added, his voice softer still.

"Do we?" Cole retorted, biting off his words almost like a snapping beast.

"I can understand your wanting to kill the man, but it's possible the brakes did fail."

"They didn't. I was there. He never went for his brakes, but just tried to bull through. Too drunk and crazy to know it couldn't be done." Cole's voice was full of fury.

"So you hated him, of course, and wanted revenge."

"I didn't say so."

"You never say much. But you act. A vanishing breed, Black called you. Quite true. But you did kill—murder—him."

"How? He was shot with an arrow, and there's no bow connected with me. Therefore it must have been somebody else. Maybe his girl stabbed him with the arrow." There was a feverish glint in the blue eyes now, as if Cole felt an urge to talk for once.

"I did some research on archery," Middlebie said in a level voice. "Many years ago, in the 1880's or so, there was often a special feature of the sport—arrow throwing. Don't bother to look surprised; you knew about it long before I did. Maybe you've known for years; more likely, finding yourself full of hate, and with only one arm, you investigated the possibilities for an archer so handicapped. It's an amazing thing, but with practice, a man could throw a special, light arrow several hundred feet."

"Try it some time," Cole said dryly.

"Oh, I can't; I know that. Few could. But you were an expert to begin with; you had the eye, the reflexes, and above all the terrible motivation. But one reason why I couldn't discover the secret for myself was the piece of string."

Cole blinked, and Middlebie knew he had struck home.

"The old archery book supplied the one vital link," he went on relentlessly. "Those long flights were accomplished mainly through an ingenious aid, related to the throwing stick used by spear men among primitive tribes. The archer—I guess we must call him that, even without a bow—ties a string to the arrow, and by tripping one end in his hand, gets a sling-like whip to his throw. That device gives the extra power needed. You didn't want to toss a light arrow several hundred feet; you wanted to send a heavy, steel headed one thirty feet, with enough force to kill. You had many months to practice, while Borden was in jail. The cabby who took you there to get a line on Borden's habits was also to be your alibi—proof that no bow was involved; just an arrow with string, hidden under your jacket."

Cole gave him a long, cool stare. Then, true to his nature, he said with slow emphasis: "You're wrong. Ask Black about the tape-recorder. All I wanted was proof that Borden never even hit the brakes. I hoped he'd say something to his girl, and I'd be able to tape it. Then I'd have the skunk cold."

"Could they try him again?" Middlebie wondered aloud. "I doubt it, and am sure you had no plans of that sort."

"There's an old Scotch motto on some university," Cole said. "Something like, 'They say. What say they? Let them say.' A nice theory, but will it hold up in court? Do you know how difficult it would be—I'm just theorizing, not having had any practice!—actually to throw an arrow thirty feet, string or no string, and split a man's spinal cord? A jury would have to see it done, and nobody in the world today can do it. I know archery, and I'm telling you."

"One man can do it," the professor said steadily.

For the first time Cole smiled—a grin of the damned.

"Will he demonstrate for the D.A.?"

Middlebie looked at him with a kind of pity. "I'm afraid not," he said in a low voice. His grey eyes fastened to the photograph on the mantel, a plump, smiling woman with happy eyes; a dark little girl, like an elf. *Maybe if I lost them*, he thought … *Well, I must tell Black, but he'll never make it stick.*

"Good night, Mr. Cole," he said gently.

The murderer gave him a silent nod.

Small, Round Man From Texas

"We don't get many European visitors around here," Sergeant Black said. He had just introduced Inspector Paul Hermite Rameau to Professor Ulysses Price Middlebie in the latter's enormous library.

"Monsieur Rameau is over here after a criminal called 'The Chameleon,' " the sergeant said, painfully conscious of his shaky French.

"Alias 'Cauchy Fourier Boussinesq,' " the inspector expanded. He was tall, for a Frenchman, and handsome. He spoke perfect English; in fact, only his too-mobile lips and glossy grooming, together with the cut of his jacket, suggested his native country. "But now, perhaps fortunately, quite dead."

"A French police official in Silver Beach," Middlebie said. Then he nodded gravely. "The big emerald robbery—right?"

"Right," Black said. "A $300,000 job, no less; and now all for the fishes, unless some skin-diver gets lucky."

"The necklace belongs to the Marquise de Tournay," Rameau said.

"The Inspector's been wanting to meet you ever since he read some of your technical stuff in the Interpol publications," the sergeant explained.

"That's very flattering," Middlebie said. "Actually my field has always been the History and Philosophy of Science; but after retiring, I got involved in the intellectual side of crime detection and found it quite stimulating."

"You would particularly find stimulation in the Chameleon," Rameau said darkly. "Boussinesq is a master of illusion through disguise. He never merely plays a part—he becomes the person in question. With his great skill in languages, and this uncanny flair for

37

mimicry, he can pass for any type from Greek to Zulu—I do not exaggerate.

"In appearance the Chameleon is striking, an odd paradox in a criminal whose forte is illusion. The man is six feet five inches tall, and very thin. How, you will ask, can such a figure be disguised? All I can say is that Boussinesq's personality is so strongly centered in the part he's playing that one simply fails to notice his build. One sees an elderly, coughing consumptive; a lathy, vigorous peasant, or even a slatternly concierge.

"So we find this thief, who specializes in jewels, making one coup after another, and always escaping by means of illusion—disguise or misdirection. He has ruined the careers of three of my predecessors, and almost did as much for mine. That he did not, I have to thank not my wits, which failed me, but the terrible Pacific surf of Silver Beach."

"And what was he doing here?" Middlebie demanded.

"He announced in France—mark the man's impudence—that he was going to steal the Marquise de Tournay's emerald necklace; that not even her visit to the United States would prevent it. So I, myself, accompanied the Marquise to California, along with my assistant, Jourdain. Your police cooperated completely; after all, the Chameleon did steal a $60,000 tiara from under the noses of the Boston detectives. He was then a high official of Ireland, which in Boston is like a license to rob banks, *hein?*

"Now you will perceive that I used the Marquise as bait, but there was no choice. She insisted on bringing the necklace, and on coming to California. I tried to dissuade her; that was my duty. When she refused, it was equally my duty, and more to my taste, to trap Boussinesq.

"We are a logical race, we French. I told my men—and your police—there are too many possible disguises. He will surely fool us again, if we play the game his way. I have an idea. There is one thing that cannot be hidden: the man's great height. We shall throw a cordon around this Silver Beach. Forget about disguise—but detain and question thoroughly everybody well over six feet in height. Once we have him in custody we can strip the Chameleon of his costume, no matter how ingenious.

"We shall even watch the sea; a patrol boat is available, and a helicopter, too. They say no small boat could possibly get through the surf at this season; but I take no chances with this *cochon*—this pig, Boussinesq."

Rameau's voice had deepened; he sat stiffly in the big armchair.

"But with all these precautions—myself, Jourdain, and the local police—he steals the necklace. A comedy of confusion involving false alarms of fire in the hotel, so that a swarm of terrified guests overwhelmed my security measures. How does one stop panicky men, women and children fleeing from the flames? No doubt one of them was tall and thin, and otherwise unremarkable—a face among many.

"This is all bad, but not unforeseen. My reliance is on sealing the town, which is done within moments after the theft. I assure you, it was impossible for the thief to escape. At three in the afternoon, the trap slammed shut. Somewhere in Silver Beach we had Boussinesq—of that, I was never in doubt.

"A search of the houses would have been tedious, but quite feasible. But, as it happened, we escaped that task. Although it was a cold, windy day, with a high surf running, the thief took to the water—a most foolish thing. We found a vital witness on one secluded beach. He was of that fanatical breed that pursues fish. He stood just before the waves with a huge rod, oh, much taller than a man, and repeatedly flung a barbed hook into the surf.

"It was he who told us of the tall, thin man who brought a bundle down to the shore, opened it, and inflated a rubber raft. And in this, the madman, none other than Boussinesq, of course, went out to sea—with a gale blowing.

"All day, even after dark, we kept our watch, and all the next day. Finally the helicopter found the empty raft, several miles out at sea—upside down. There was nobody aboard, or clinging to it. Clearly the Chameleon had drowned, taking the necklace with him to the bottom, one presumes."

Middlebie's shaggy eyebrows rose, and Black, knowing him, guessed that the old man's imaginative mind was frenetically active; one could visualize computer lights flashing.

At that moment the phone rang. At the professor's nod, Black answered it.

"For you, Inspector," he said, holding the instrument out to their visitor.

"*Allo. Oui*, Inspector Rameau. Jourdain—*quoi?* What are you saying? *Mais*, it is impossible—unbelievable!" He added some hasty instructions and hung up. When he turned back to Middlebie, his eyes showed a pathetic kind of bewilderment.

"I do not understand. Already one of the emeralds has turned up with a—what is that word?—fence. Yes, a fence. After only four days—and the Chameleon dead. Could he have left it with somebody? But no; that wasn't his method …"

"Inspector," the professor asked softly. "This witness—the fisherman on the beach. You went over his story?"

"But of course. He was a boor—a fanatic, as I said. All the time fishing; he would not even turn to me; no, I had to move in front, and dodge his great pole. There he stood, like a tree, with big feet planted wide, tossing out that silly hook. After I left, he stayed until dark, my men told me, in that freezing wind—and catching nothing, *naturellement*."

"What did he look like?"

"A small, round man—on vacation—from Texas, he said."

For a moment the professor seemed about to speak, and Black felt a little stir of excitement. But Middlebie only expressed sympathy, and then changed the subject completely.

It was only after Rameau had left that the old man unburdened himself.

"It's clear why the emeralds are turning up," he said. "Because obviously Boussinesq isn't dead; he never went to sea at all."

"Wha-at?" The sergeant was incredulous. "The witness couldn't have known him, and yet the description is exact."

"Illusion again," Middlebie said dryly. "The witness was Boussinesq."

"Hold on! Face, yes; or clothes; but you can't make a tall, skinny man into a short, round one."

"The roundness was padding; that's simple, and the easiest part of the illusion. Remember, the man didn't move *until after dark*."

"What does that mean?" Black demanded. "Would moving change his build?"

"Let me show how. Before stealing the gems, Boussinesq hides a few props on the beach. One of his props is the raft; the other, I'd stake my life, is a gimmicked pair of waders."

"Gimmicked how?"

"Rameau mentioned the man's big feet—which he never shifted until after dark. I suppose he took a pair of waders, removed the soles, and merely passed his legs through—into holes dug in the sand. His feet and about eight inches of lower leg were buried, and above them, pressing apparently on the solid beach, were the sole-less empty ends of the boots.

"All right; after misdirecting the Inspector, Boussinesq continues casting until dark. Then he slips out of the trick waders, buries them, and leaves the area. In the dim light, they can't see his height; no doubt he crouches to make sure. Then he hides until the roadblocks are lifted when the upturned raft is sighted. The man's a genius, Black!"

"Why didn't you tell Rameau?"

"I didn't have the heart—then." He sighed. "But I guess we'll have to before he goes back. Maybe next time the Chameleon won't fool him."

"Wanna bet?" Black said, grinning widely.

41

Blood Will Tell

"Breathes there a cop with hide so tough, he thinks four amendments aren't enough!"

Ulysses Price Middlebie, former Professor Emeritus of the History and Philosophy of Science, and sometime consultant in criminology, smiled tightly at Sergeant Black's doggerel. "The Fifth Amendment," he said solemnly, "is a splendid conception, designed to prevent the taking of evidence under torture. It is no more to be blamed for being misused than the morphine which, instead of helping a cancer victim, gives some young fool a thrill."

"I know," Black said. "I was just letting off steam. It's damned frustrating to see a murderer get off scot-free, no matter how noble the Fifth Amendment itself might be. Besides, it isn't always clear to us cops just how the lawyers spread that one rule so ludicrously thin."

Middlebie sank deeper into his old leather armchair, and fixed luminous grey eyes on the young detective.

"I'm not a lawyer," he said, "so it's not at all plain to me what you expect here. In the purely scientific matters of crime detection, I've been able to help you out on several occasions. But if you're looking for loopholes in the Fifth Amendment, I must plead a total incapacity to offer advice."

"You have a point," Black admitted. "It's just that you are a problem-solver, and even though a legal aspect is involved, there may be some other approach I can't visualize. You might be able to succeed, judging from past performance. In any case, I'd like to discuss the situation with you—okay?"

"By all means. Your cases are usually quite interesting. Or possibly you don't bring me the other kind."

"That's right, I don't. I come to you only when I'm in a bind. I'm a pretty good detective," he added, without false modesty, "but you've made a specialty of logical deduction, and have fifty years of experience in practicing what you preach. I know it wasn't crime consultations, but more of a PhD Doctor—a man who could help almost any young research student over a bad block in his project. There isn't such a difference. Your work on past cases proves that."

"Thanks," Middlebie said dryly. "But any more butter, and I'll need a serum cholesterol test!" Then he smiled in a way that removed any sting from the reproach. "I know you meant that as a sincere compliment, but it's difficult for an old curmudgeon like me to accept praise gracefully. Now, about the case—or rather," he punned outrageously, "the fifth!"

"Well, it's basically a simple matter. There's a skunk by the name of Carleton Chambers Dell—at least, that's his current one—who has almost certainly disposed of three wives for their insurance and possessions. They were murdered in other states, by the way. Now he's killed a fourth one here, and luckily for us, got a little careless. It seems that wife number four got in a good swing at his nose, which is hard to miss, and he spilled several ounces of blood at the scene of the crime. It was meant to look like an accident, but he goofed, and the death was called murder."

He paused, and Middlebie asked: "Where does the Fifth Amendment come in? It would seem to be a clear case of First Degree Homicide."

"Ordinarily, yes, but Dell has the luck of the Devil. There are several possible suspects he didn't know existed, but we turned them up—not with any intention of helping him, you can bet! Just part of the routine investigation before we even knew about Dell's past record. In other words, we don't have a sure case against him—one that will really stand up in court, and against his lawyer, who's about the best around. As to the Fifth Amendment, did you know that it applies in this state to a blood test? That is, we can't force Dell to give us a sample of his blood. That pool near the victim undoubtedly came from his nose, which was known to be red and bruised the morning after the murder. It's the rarest type, the police lab says, and if we could state in court that Dell's blood is a match, I think we'd have him, because the other suspects are all different."

"I should think the elimination ought to be enough," Middlebie said.

"Not with Parks, his lawyer. He'll bring in another unknown killer and confuse the issue. Mrs. Dell was a weird one, and had a lot of offbeat friends. One of them *might* have done it."

"Are you sure it didn't happen that way?"

"Morally, yes, because of his past record. But we can't use that during the trial; that's never permitted. Plus the fact that he's obviously scared to death about giving any blood. He's claimed everything from religious objections—and he has about as much religion as the late Stalin—down to the Fifth Amendment. That did it. The court has warned us not to touch his sacred veins, or else."

"I suppose," Middlebie said, a wicked glint in his eyes, "you couldn't manage to have somebody, quite casually, punch his nose in public?"

"I thought of that," Black admitted ruefully. "But we'd be crucified in court. They'd make a martyr out of Dell. Too many complaints about abuse of police power these days. Some of it is justified," he added hastily, "but cops are human, and they like shortcuts as well as the next guy. When you see some punk sneering at the law, and practically daring you to make something stick, it's hard to remember civil liberties. That's not an excuse; just an explanation."

"We should all be careful about criticizing anybody until we've worn his shoes a few days," Middlebie said. "But surely Dell must have an army record, complete with blood type."

"Not that we can find. My guess is he ducked that one just as easily as he's ducked the law. Hid out in Mexico, faked a disease, or got an 'essential' job through bribery or pull—who knows?"

"What about hospitalization?"

"Nothing. Either he's in perfect health, or, more likely, used a phony name. So you see what I'm up against. No blood, no solid case. Either I let him go without bringing a murder charge, or pull him in, and risk losing in court because there's no proof that blood came from his big, bunged-up nose."

Middlebie was silent for a moment, his eyes blank. After a few moments he said: "Then I take it that if—and mind you I only say 'if'; I don't know how it could be done—but if you could get some of his blood without violence, even through fraud, you'd have your case."

"Provided we could prove in court our sample really came from Dell. Which means good, dependable medical evidence in the form of some reputable doctor." Black's face was grim. "It's a hopeless problem. Blood without violence. He's so cautious now that if Albert Schweitzer wanted to nick him for any reason, Dell would refuse automatically. Nobody's going to get any of his blood voluntarily, that's certain. And we can't take it by force. So I guess I've bent your ear for nothing. The problem can't have a solution."

"At the moment, I'd have to agree," the professor said. "But let me sleep on it. Occasionally an impossible problem has an obvious answer."

Black looked at him in wonder.

"You mean there might be a chance?" He shook his head several times. "You never say 'die,' do you? Well, I know better than to bet against you, but I can't see a way out of this mess." He paused at the door. "Here's hoping I hear from you tomorrow."

"Wonderful stuff, blood," Middlebie said absently. "No wonder so many people hate the idea of losing any. I don't mean criminals, like Dell," he added. Then, with more resolution in his voice, "We can't let this wife killer get away with only a punch in the nose!"

"He will, if you don't stop him," Black retorted, and left.

When he was gone, the professor prepared a swig of his pet drink, a loathsome brew made up of bourbon, brown sugar, and bock beer. He sipped this with relish while reading a long article on the subject of blood. It told him more than he wanted to know, and none of the information promised to be of use in Black's dilemma. Until the part about sporozoan parasites …

Late the next night, Middlebie, Sergeant Black, and a small, round querulous man, known the world over as an authority on tropical

45

medicine, moved with the air of conspirators up to the rear window of a certain motel apartment.

"This is the one," Black whispered.

"You're sure?" Middlebie husked in his very low monotone.

"Positive. Dell's asleep in there right now. You ready, Dr. Forrest?"

The small man said in a deep, frog-like croak, "Of course, I'm ready. But if anybody except Middlebie asked me to participate in such a fool's trick—and in the middle of the night!" His voice faded away in an irritable mutter.

Quietly, with almost surgical skill, Black made a hole in the screen. It was a warm night, and the window was up several inches. A word from Middlebie, and Forrest held something over the hole. When he removed it some moments later, the sergeant stuffed cotton into the opening. Then the three men retreated.

"Two detectives will watch the place until morning," Black said, as they got to the car. "As soon as it's light, I'll pick Dell up and, of course, I need you there too. My men can prove nobody else went into the room, but you'll have to vouch for the rest. It's going to work," he said gleefully. "It's got to!"

FROM THE TRIAL RECORD:
The State Vs.
Carleton Chambers Dell

STATE'S ATTORNEY BRAND: Please tell the court, in your own words, Professor Middlebie, just what happened on the night of June 18th. Be as explicit as possible.

MIDDLEBIE: Dr. Forrest, Sergeant Black, and myself went to the Sea Foam Motel, found the rear window of the defendant's apartment, and cut a small hole in the screen. Through it, Dr. Forrest released fifty common mosquitoes, all with empty stomachs, and all dyed bright yellow with a harmless chemical pigment.

BRAND: Would you explain those points—about the empty stomachs, and the dye?

MIDDLEBIE: Certainly. Those female mosquitoes—the only kind that bite—were raised in the laboratory, in wire cages, for Dr. Forrest's

46

work in parasitology. Consequently, any blood found in their stomachs in the morning must necessarily have come from the one warm-blooded inhabitant of that motel room. As for the dye, that insured our using only those insects released by us. That is, there was no chance of our capturing any—ah—mavericks that might have brought blood from somebody other than the defendant.

BRAND: I see. And in the morning, you did subsequently recapture some of the dyed mosquitoes?

MIDDLEBIE: Yes, from the walls of the motel room. The blood in their stomachs was typed, both by Dr. Forrest and police technicians.

BRAND: As to that, further testimony will show the blood to be of the relatively rare type spilled by the murderer in the victim's room …

"I never saw a more surprised man than Dell," Black said later. "The jury was flabbergasted enough, but Dell!—I almost felt sorry for him. The jury couldn't disregard the words of men like you and Forrest. And how could *we* be blamed for the mosquitoes' 'force and violence'?"

"There's a certain subtle justice you may have overlooked," Professor Middlebie said. "Not only did Dell have a miserable night, what with fifty starved mosquitoes in that small place, but all his torture and the murder conviction—came from the females of the species."

Coffee Break

"I always thought that locked room cases occurred only in detective novels." Sergeant Black's tone was plaintive, as if he accused the universe of unfairness to the police.

Ulysses Price Middlebie, object of the remark, and former Professor of the History and Philosophy of Science, but now a sometime crime consultant, looked thoughtful.

"Undoubtedly they began with mystery fiction," he said evenly. "But life does imitate art. To put it otherwise, I'm sure that many bright and imaginative crimes have been suggested—even guided step by step—by ingenious stories."

"Which means in addition to out-guessing dumb apes with lengths of pipe, we now have to keep two jumps ahead of the best mystery story writers!" the sergeant grumbled. "I don't suppose *you* ever read such stuff," he added.

"To the contrary," Middlebie said. "I've always enjoyed a good crime story, especially of the puzzle variety. And now even more so." He glanced down at his heavily taped ankle, which was propped up on a hassock.

"As much my bad luck as yours," Black said. "It's the kind of case where you'd come in very handy. But you can't get around, even to watch birds, and anything that stops you from galloping over hill and dale with binoculars is pretty bad."

"Tell me about it, anyhow," Middlebie suggested. "I may still be of some help." Then he added dryly: "My head isn't taped."

Black had the grace to redden slightly.

"You're right of course," he said. "It's your brains I've picked, mostly. But you must admit," he persisted, "that often I just miss seeing things that are significant to you because of your scientific background."

"True, but I'll try to pry out of you even the things you saw without noticing them. So go ahead, and give me all the facts."

The sergeant paused to organize his thoughts for a moment, and then began the recital.

"The dead man is Cyrus Denning, a bachelor of sixty-two. He's supposed to have poisoned himself with cyanide. His prints, and only his, are on the cup. He was found dead in a locked room. Nobody had been near him for at least half an hour before his death. From here on in," Black suggested, "we'd better change to that method—Socratic, wasn't it?—you liked so much in college, because I don't really know what to tell you or in what order."

"All right," the professor said amiably. "That's as good an approach as any. You say the door was locked. How?"

"Bolted on the inside; a heavy brass bolt."

"That's not such an impossibility. Such a door can often be locked by attaching a string or wire to the bolt, and shooting it home from the outside."

"Not this time," Black said grimly. "The door is recessed, and fits too tightly. Besides, no such string was found, and my suspect had no chance to remove it."

"Very well. What about a window?"

"One, at the back. It's been nailed shut for years, and undisturbed; that I guarantee. I went over every inch with a good magnifying glass."

"Could the glass have been cut out and re-puttied in?" There was a twinkle in the old man's grey eyes. "That's one from a mystery story I read some months ago."

"Not a prayer. It was old, crumbly putty; dry and hard, but still holding tight."

"Why nailed down?"

"Denning didn't care much about fresh air, and he was very secretive. Fancied himself a scientist and inventor. The place was a one room cabin by Lake Bradley, converted into a workroom and lab. The front door—the only one—he used to padlock on the outside when he left. When he was working there, he usually bolted it from the inside."

Middlebie frowned slightly. "Perhaps I should ask why, in the face of all this, you doubt he killed himself."

Black's lips narrowed. "Instinct—plus the fact that he left no note. In my experience, a suicide almost always leaves some explanation. Then there's the fact that Denning was filthy rich. When there's enough money as bait, the greedy rats can be inferred."

"Do you have a particular rodent in mind?"

"You bet. The old man's nephew. He was right there when they found him, and he's the lad to inherit two hundred thousand bucks, and who knows how to spend it fast."

"So he was at the cabin. Let's have the details."

"The boy—his name's Jerry Doss—admits seeing his uncle in the lab at noon. Sometimes he helped Denning, and managed to borrow a few bucks each time; not much because the old boy was tighter than a new girdle.

"Anyhow, he left Denning at 1:30, alive, he claims. The old man promptly bolted the door behind him. Then Doss went across the lake—that's about a hundred yards—to chat for a bit with the man at the dock, who rents boats in season. Things are quiet there now, of course.

"Well, he stayed there for half an hour, then left. But he asked the boatman to keep an eye on Denning's front door, which to me is one sign of a plot. The boy was obviously setting up an alibi."

"What reason did he give for such an odd request?"

"He told the fellow that Denning had been bothered by some of the kids—that they hammered at the door and ragged him. Doss said that if the boatman could catch them at it, and identify them, his uncle would be glad to slip him ten bucks."

"Very plausible," Middlebie said, with a wry grin. "The boy has imagination—*if* he invented the story."

"I'm betting he did. Anyhow, at this point all is clear. Doss left Denning half an hour before, and didn't go near the door, as the boatman can testify. He never took his eyes off the area, watching for the kids, and hoping to earn ten bucks the easy way.

"Then, about fifteen minutes after the boy left the dock, the man sees him at the front door, hammering away and yelling. Finally, he turns and motions to the boatman to join him. When the guy gets there, Doss tells him that he looked in the window, and saw that his uncle was either dead or unconscious. The window's in back, remember, so nobody could have seen the boy look in."

"Well, they break down the door—it takes both of them, because of the heavy brass bolt—and find Denning dead, with a cup of poison at his hand. He's slumped over the table near the window."

"Couldn't he have been killed when Doss first left? Before going across the lake to the boatman?"

"That's what bugs me," Black groaned. "There was a cup of coffee on the table, boiling hot. It must have been recently poured—and that's where the cyanide was. Cold water wasn't good enough for this suicide. He has to have his poison in fresh, hot coffee!"

"And that isn't all," the detective almost shrieked. "A cigarette was burning on the edge of an ash tray. It couldn't have been lit more than a few minutes earlier." He looked at the professor, his whole face one agonized question mark.

"Hmmm," Middlebie murmured. "I begin to see what you're upset about."

"So it has to be suicide, and I'm an idiot," Black said, more quietly, "only I don't like the smirk of that nephew, or the little spark in his beady eyes. He engineered this deal some way, and I want to nail him!"

The professor was lost in thought for the moment. Then he said absently: "You must have read about Sherlock Holmes."

Black gaped at him.

"I'm thinking of his brother, Mycroft," Middlebie said, smiling.

"Mycroft?"

"Like me, he was immobilized. In his case, sheer laziness and bulk. But he solved some very puzzling cases from his armchair, with brother Sherlock doing the leg work." He gave Black a quizzical stare. "Why don't we try that, eh?"

"I'll try anything," the sergeant said. "I'm good at leg work. Sometimes I think that's all I'm good at."

"Nonsense. You have brains and imagination," the professor assured him in a gruff voice. "Now, here's what I'd like you to do. Get me large, clear photos of the lab, inside and out, all four sides. And of the view from the place in all directions." His eyes clouded briefly, and he said: "Are you sure the bolt is brass, and not just painted that color?"

"Painted? No, but why—" He bit the question off short. "I'll certainly find out," he promised, his voice hard.

"You do that, and let me know. Is there a phone in the lab?"

"Yes."

"Then call me from there. And bring the pictures as soon as they're available."

"I'll phone you in three hours. We should have pictures by tomorrow afternoon."

"Good." Middlebie watched the sergeant stride to the door. When Black had left, the old man opened a drawer in his desk, took out a fifth of bourbon, and after some painful limping about, made his favorite tipple of whisky, beer, and brown sugar. He sipped it appreciatively, his brow knitting with thought every few moments.

Two hours and forty-eight minutes later Black phoned.

"The bolt seems to be brass," he said. "At least, it's not iron, steel, aluminum, or lead."

"Hmph," Middlebie said, his voice indicating some disappointment. "That's a pity." After a moment's silence, he spoke again, his tone sharper. "I want you to scrape that bolt all over, and study it with that magnifying glass you were bragging about. Call me back if you spot anything interesting."

"What am I looking for?" the sergeant demanded irritably.

"Just make a careful examination and see what develops," the professor said. And he hung up.

Half an hour later, Black called back; there was a hum of excitement in his voice.

"I don't know how you knew," he said, "but somebody's been at the bolt, all right. Looks as if he drilled a hole, and put in a plug of some kind."

"Ahh," Middlebie purred. "Soft iron, I'll bet anything. First hypothesis verified."

"What's it all about?" Black queried eagerly.

"Tell you when we get those pictures," the professor said. "Bring 'em over tomorrow, will you?"

"Damn right, I will. But tell me—"

"Tomorrow," was the firm reply. "It's not all clear yet. Not at all." Again he hung up.

The next day, early in the afternoon, the sergeant appeared with a stack of glossy eight by tens. Middlebie took them, and shuffled through the pile in an impatient way, finally fishing out a shot of the interior. He peered at it, and groaned.

"S'matter?" Black demanded.

"The table." Middlebie's voice was full of disgust. "It's too far from the window. If only it had been right next to it … I don't suppose," he said wistfully, "there was any way to introduce the coffee and cigarette after the door was bolted."

"None," the sergeant declared. "Oh, there is a chimney from the fireplace, but I'd like to see the man dexterous enough to get a nearly full cup of hot coffee and a lighted cigarette down that. And with the chimney in plain sight of Wilson—he's the boatman."

"Another good theory gone to pot," the professor said. Then he asked: "By the way, was the coffee pot also hot?"

"Had to be," Black said. "It was still on a tiny gas fire."

Middlebie shook his head in admiration.

"That killer, whoever he was—and *if* he was—has brains. Pity he's warped. The lad even avoided anybody's finding a discrepancy between boiling hot coffee in a cup, and a pot only lukewarm. He just left the coffee on the flame—damned foresighted."

A bit dubious now, he studied the pictures. Suddenly his gaze grew sharp.

"What's that behind the cabin—this thing on the pillar. It looks like an astronomical telescope."

"That's just what it is," the sergeant said. "Denning dabbled in astronomy, too. They say he even found a new comet."

"This seems to be a refractor."

"Could be. I didn't pay much attention."

"You'd better pay more. I want the name of the manufacturer. But don't touch it; there may be prints."

"Whose prints? And what difference? I wish I knew what was going on in your head these last few days." The sergeant was obviously exasperated.

"I'll tell you when I'm sure myself," the old man soothed him. "Wouldn't want you to think I'm senile. Be a good lad, and check that scope. Get the maker's name, and if that isn't on it, measure the diameter of the objective—the big lens at the end. But hands off. Got it?"

"All right," Black said. Then he smiled briefly. "… Mycroft!"

Middlebie blinked. That was the first time the sergeant had ever dared come back at him. Good! It was time they had a less formal relationship.

"Before I go," Black said, gazing directly into the grey eyes, "please explain that bit about the bolt. Certainly you're sure of that part."

"Oh, yes. I didn't mean to conceal anything," the professor said. "Open that right hand cabinet, and take out what's on the second shelf up."

The sergeant obeyed him, and was amazed at his own former incomprehension.

"Right," Middlebie said. "That's a magnet; a big one. It weighs five pounds, and has a two thousand gauss rating. Which means, I would guess, that even through a thick wooden door it has enough pull on a bit of iron imbedded in a brass bolt to slide the thing into its socket. Did you notice if the assembly was smooth working—oiled, perhaps?"

"You bet it was!" Black exclaimed. "So that's it. What a chump I've been. All Doss had to do was step out, shut the door on his dead uncle, and move this kind of magnet from left to right at the proper height against the door." He flipped the piece of heavy metal from hand to hand in his enthusiasm. Then his face darkened. "But we're still up the creek on that coffee and cigarette bit. We know he was away from the cabin for over half an hour. The coffee would have cooled by then, and the smoke gone out."

"I am aware of the difficulty," the professor said. "That's why I hoped the table would be nearer the window. By the way," he asked, "what kind of a day was it—the weather, I mean?"

"Nice one; cool, clear, sunny. Anybody but an old idiot would have been outside, or at least had a window open to enjoy the fresh air."

"It takes all kinds," Middlebie said. "Go check on that telescope like a good lad."

Black seemed about to ask more questions, but the old man's face was forbiddingly wooden. With a sigh, the detective left.

When he returned that evening, Middlebie was working with a binocular microscope, and seemed almost reluctant to shift his line of thought. He shoved his chair back, gave a grunt of resignation, and raised one eyebrow questioningly.

"Well?" he demanded.

"No maker's name that I could find. But the objective was five inches across."

"Good. A five incher could have a focal length of from sixty to ninety inches."

"What does that mean?" Black's voice was querulous. He was tired of driving up and back, and almost sorry he hadn't certified the case as suicide. Only sheer persistence—plus the nature of a good cop—made him stay with it.

"Here's how it must have happened," Middlebie said, sounding the least bit smug. "Doss visits his uncle; maybe works with him a bit in the lab. Then they have coffee, either as normal routine, or at the boy's suggestion. There are cases of standard chemicals against the south wall; your pictures show them plainly. It's easy for Doss to put cyanide in the old man's cup. The moment his uncle collapsed, the boy wiped his own prints off the cup, pressed Denning's on, and left, closing the door behind him. But first he put an unlighted cigarette on the edge of the ceramic ash tray.

"Once outside, he unobtrusively—in case somebody was watching—stood facing the door, and with a magnet taken probably from his uncle's lab, shot the bolt. I assume that at some earlier visit, when left alone by the old man, he drilled out some of the brass and inserted an iron plug so the magnet would work.

"Now, then. He went to the dock and established that half hour alibi. After that, Doss approached the cabin from the rear, where neither the boatman nor anybody else could see him, took the objective glass—already loosened, I imagine, the boy being so thorough—and stood a foot or two from the window. There, he focused the bright sunlight—"

"By God!" Black exclaimed, almost in a whisper, and Middlebie frowned at the interruption.

"An ordinary magnifier wouldn't work unless the table was only inches from the glass, but this thing focuses at from sixty to ninety inches. The window glass would cut a lot of the heat, but there would be plenty to bring the coffee cup to boiling, and then light the cigarette.

"Then, very quickly, to the front door, there to pound and finally hail the boatman. Very neat!"

"You've got it," Black said. "No doubt of that." He shook his head gloomily. "But how to prove anything in court?"

"Well," the old man said. "The drilled bolt has some evidential value."

"Not enough, I'm afraid."

"Prints on the telescope?"

"Weak," the sergeant said crisply. "After all, the boy helped out in the scientific stuff."

"Ah," Middlebie said. "But if you're lucky, there'll be some on the *inside* of the objective. They would be harder to explain; much harder, since few astronomers ever dismount the objective. There are realignment problems, and dust—all sorts of reasons to leave it alone. But frankly, I think if you go at it right, the boy may crack. He doesn't dream we're onto him. Feeling plenty smug, I imagine."

Black looked at the lean face and seemed to see cats' whiskers twitching.

He's not the only one who feels that way, the sergeant reflected with amusement. But aloud he said only, "In any case, you've done your share. No Mycroft could have done better."

A Model Crime

"A hundred and thirty to the ounce—and each one worth up to twenty dollars, with no questions asked! And over eight ounces have disappeared without a trace!"

"Almost as compact and valuable as dope," Professor Middlebie said thoughtfully, shifting his bandaged ankle to a softer spot on the hassock. "Ironical, in a way, that two things so different in purpose and consumption should share such qualities as lightness and high cost. Are you sure of those figures?" he demanded, head cocked, grey eyes steady. "They seem a bit remarkable, even for transistors, small as they are."

"I'm giving it to you just as I heard it," Sergeant Black said, looking slightly hurt at the suggestion that he, of all people, was a fallible witness. "They're like pinheads, with two hair wires coming out. Precision made; custom made; you ought to see the place. Dust-free, air pressure inside so that nothing can blow in; and all the technicians wear lintless coveralls."

"Well," Middlebie said, "if you want me to try another Mycroft— we didn't do too badly on that locked room murder a few weeks ago, at that," he interjected with just a trace of complacency—"I'm willing. Maybe I should quit while I'm ahead. Armchair deduction is chancy stuff, with a big element of luck. But, frankly, I'm sick of being immobilized, especially with all the migrants flying through the valley." He shot a wistful glance at his binoculars, lying on the sill of the old fashioned bay window.

"Good," Black said. Then a rather puzzled expression crossed his face. "You know," he said slowly, "I've taken you at your word—I mean as to your qualities. I've thought of you as the scientist who coldly, logically, examines all the possible hypotheses that account for the tricky facts, and then selects the best one—presumably the only one—after which I do the final leg work to get legal evidence." He paused, and the professor, once a lecturer on the History and Philosophy of Science, and now an occasional crime consultant for his former pupil, raised a pair of bushy eyebrows.

"And now you have another opinion?" the older man asked.

"In a way. Sure, you see everything with a naturalist's eye, and you have the scientific background to interpret all the data. But," he added triumphantly, "basically it's your imagination that's so good! Forming those hypotheses is a matter of invention, speculation. The fact is, Professor, you're as much an artist as a scientist."

"Thank you," Middlebie said dryly. "The most casual study of past discoveries in science would have taught you that with much less effort on your part. Every successful investigator has had to have as much imagination as technical skill. Once you come up with a really brilliant idea—like Mendel's, or Einstein's—any one of hundreds, with no imaginations of their own, can check it out. But while you're working out a philosophy of science," he added, smiling, "those transistors are getting farther away every minute."

"Ouch!" Black said. "Here's the story, brief and to the point.

"Three days ago, at Morton Electronics, eight ounces of transistors turned up missing. The company can't make 'em fast enough to satisfy the demand. They're the best available, custom-built by the finest technicians around. Morton uses most of them in its own products, but whenever there's a surplus—usually very small—they sell the transistors alone. The going price is twenty dollars each. So eight ounces, at a hundred and thirty to the ounce, are worth about twenty-one thousand dollars—quite a haul. Besides, on the black market, the thief might get as much as fifty thousand.

"The factory makes a lot of valuable stuff—the best oscilloscopes, special radio receivers, things for satellites—small items that are worth a lot of money. So they're careful; they have to be. Nobody takes anything out, and even what they bring in is inspected—don't ask me why."

"I could think of one reason already," Middlebie said with a kind of boyish glee.

"What's that?"

"A catapult, or crossbow—to shoot a package of transistors fifty or a hundred yards away from the building, to be picked up later."

"Say-y-y," the sergeant said, "that's damned good." Then he shook his head. "But it wouldn't work. It's a big plant; you'd have to shoot a couple of blocks to get anything from the factory to the nearest fence—which is twelve feet high, topped by barbed wire, guarded day and night, and floodlit, too!"

"How dependable are the guards?"

"The best. You may have heard of the Safeguard Organization. They've never had a crook working for them. Their men are gradually given more responsibility and top wages. Nothing doing there. Oh, we're checking, too, but I don't expect any weak links."

"All right," Middlebie said, "since we're back with the Socratic method again, let me ask you this. Are all the people who work in the factory possible suspects?"

"No, luckily. Only five men—the chief engineers of various departments—have access to the room where the transistors were stolen. The other employees sign for every item of that sort from supply."

"Tell me about the chosen five."

"Well, they're high-paid experts, naturally. Each has a private office."

"Really private?"

"So I gathered," Black said. "The doors can be locked, and often are, since some of the engineers keep secret and very valuable blueprints handy. They're often working on special projects of their own. Some of the offices are almost like labs."

"Secretaries come in and out, surely."

"Some have to knock first, unless they've been rung for. You know how these young geniuses act at times. If they don't want to be bothered, even the president of the company may cool his heels outside."

Middlebie was silent for a moment, a cloudy look in his eyes.

"No chance, I take it, of smuggling the transistors out."

"None," Black said crisply. "A complete change of clothes before leaving. Maybe the president is exempt—I didn't check that—but nobody else."

"Could they have gone out in small batches?"

"No. It was easy to pin down the time. All eight ounces were taken Wednesday night."

"You mean they work such hours?"

"Around the clock. As I said, they can't turn out the stuff fast enough, and the overtime pay could buy a nuclear submarine."

"Hmmph!" the professor said, a narrow furrow appearing in his brow. "Could they still be hidden in the plant anywhere?"

"I don't see how. The place is on a dust-free routine, so that everything is rounded, smooth, polished, and cleaned a million times a week. There simply are no lockers, cabinets, or the like—they'd be bad dust catchers. The factory's like one big tiled bathroom—or even more like the inside of a refrigerator, with the shelves and gadgets out."

"This would send even Mycroft's blood pressure up," Middlebie said ruefully. "Maybe that's why Holmes consulted him only a few times—two, I think. What about the five suspects? Did all of them go to the supply room that day?"

"Unfortunately, yes."

"And were all of them out of sight when the transistors disappeared?"

"Fortunately, no. Two were with colleagues or secretaries."

"So, really, there are just three main suspects."

"I suppose so." Black sounded doubtful. "It's not that clear-cut. Maybe even with others around somebody had a clever way to work it. How can I say, without the faintest idea to start on?"

"Well," the professor said judiciously, "I think it's time for the essential leg work. Even Mycroft needed Sherlock's data to accomplish anything."

"Fine," Black said in a somewhat sour voice. "What do I look for?"

"Anything unusual that anybody might have seen, heard, felt, smelled, or inferred psychologically. That includes people—especially children, who are the most curious of individuals—who live near the plant."

"How about the ones overhead?" the sergeant suggested, his voice even more sour.

"Overhead? What do you mean?"

"A plane flies over the factory every night at 8:45—it's bound for San Francisco, from Los Angeles"—here Black's tone became a singsong chant—"with a crew of five, and forty passengers. It flies at twelve thousand feet at a speed of—"

"I get the point," Middlebie said. "You don't feel that they let down a rope for the loot, nor do you suspect they swooped low the way planes picked up agents in enemy territory during the war—hooking a man off the ground in a harness."

"If you—" the sergeant began, but the professor, still smiling, continued.

"Nor do you believe they could have seen or heard anything in the dark at twelve thousand feet. Do you know what I think?"

"What?" Black was thoroughly bewildered.

"I agree one hundred percent." Then, in a serious voice, "But please ask around as I suggested, and then report back. Meanwhile, I'll use that imagination you overly praised a few minutes ago. Before you go, get me a beer from the refrigerator. I need some high-test brain fuel."

As Black left, the professor was mixing the horrible tipple he favored: beer, whisky, and brown sugar—called by some, Bullfrog Gin; drink a little, hop a little, and croak.

He sipped the concoction, gave a small sigh of pleasure, and gave his imagination free rein. A guarded factory; a competent engineer; eight ounces of treasure sent through, around, or over all barriers—how? Middlebie began to jot down some possible answers …

When Black returned the following evening, he had nothing to report. Nobody had seen or heard a thing, except for the regularly scheduled plane already mentioned.

"We're not going to get any eyewitnesses, that's certain," the sergeant said gloomily. "And not much evidence of any kind. Talk about a case for pure reason, this is it in spades!"

"Let's plug a few more holes," Middlebie told him. "What about the stuff being shipped out in some routine consignment—radios, amplifiers, that sort of thing."

"I thought of that. They inspect everything several times—performance tests, completeness, the works. Besides, the engineers have no direct dealings with the shipping room, and if one of them had been around there, even for a minute, we'd know about it."

"All right. Then, this: what's the size of an eight-ounce parcel of transistors?"

"Fairly bulky. They're sealed in little plastic pods to keep out air, dust—anything that might hurt 'em. I'm told the crook must have carried out a package about the size of a cigarette carton—maybe a bit smaller, if the things were compressed."

"That's very interesting," the professor said. "It means almost certainly that they weren't taken out on the thief's person; not with the kind of inspection you described. So I'm back, oddly enough, to my first rather wild speculations. Never underrate intuition, my boy."

"I don't follow you," Black said.

"Sherlock Holmes had a dictum, often discussed, to the effect that when one has eliminated the impossible, whatever remains, however improbable, is the answer. The rule actually avoids the main difficulty, for who is qualified to know when *all* the impossible solutions have been considered? That little word 'all' has bedeviled logicians for centuries." Then, seeing the sergeant's glassy stare, he added, "Sorry. All I mean is that we're narrowing down the number of reasonable solutions."

"So that's *all* you mean," Black grinned. "That word again!"

Middlebie ignored him.

"I need more data," he said briskly. "Find out what kind of equipment each suspect has in his office, particularly if there's anything for metal working, like a jeweler's lathe, or the like. And then"—here the sergeant groaned—"get me the most complete dossier possible on each engineer, going well back in time."

"Like how many times they asked to be excused in third grade?"

"If the information is available," was the bland reply.

Black didn't delve quite that deeply, but after a week he brought back a thick folder on each man. The professor read each one through with great patience, missing very little. Finally, in a high school yearbook—how in the world had Black come up with that?—he found something concrete.

"By the way, on that equipment question," he asked the sergeant. "Does Brenner have a lathe in his office?"

"No," was the prompt reply. "A lot of electronic stuff, and plenty of tools, but nothing to turn metal."

"You're sure? It might be inside the desk."

"It isn't. And in addition, he never had one. I checked that on my own," Black said reproachfully.

"Do they use any gasoline in the plant?"

"Not that I know of. They have a special solvent for cleaning parts, though."

"Hmmph." The professor's expression suggested he was at a dead end. "No metal; that means no engine, even with gas available." He held out the yearbook. "See that?"

Black studied the blurry photo, and his jaw muscles knotted.

He said: "You think—but that's impossible!"

"That's a model plane, and the yearbook mentions how far advanced young Brenner was in that field, back in '45. Yet, in these recent biographical notes you and your men made, he never said a word about such a hobby. Why should he hide it now?"

"Maybe he just outgrew it."

"Maybe. We'll see." Middlebie pointed to a shelf. "Get me that thick, reddish book."

The sergeant did so, and the old man riffled the pages. Then he stabbed one triumphantly.

"Aha! Who won third place for endurance only eight years ago? R. T. Brenner. And was the plane radio-controlled? You bet your sweet life!"

"But—but—" Black sounded like an outboard motor gone wild. "You said no lathe, no motor, no gas—"

"Right. But Brenner's an *electrical* engineer. Nowadays, with new cadmium batteries, you can fly a plane pretty well by electric motor.

Remember, he didn't need more than a few hundred yards, and he probably left off any landing gear. Just over the fence, out into the dark, and then ..." He paused for a moment, as if in doubt.

"And then?" the sergeant prompted eagerly.

"He could have had an accomplice, but I think not. These papers"—patting the dossier—"suggest he's always been a lone wolf. My guess is he just crashed the plane out there at some convenient spot. Is there any open ground, fairly isolated, around the plant?"

"Only to the east. Fifty acres of scrub-bush, gullies, and rattlesnakes—just the thing for a new housing development."

"Then look for traces there."

Black gaped at him.

"Look, sir, you know he couldn't possibly have carried in a model plane big enough to fly eight ounces over a thousand yards."

"Of course not." Middlebie sounded annoyed. "Obviously he built the plane at intervals in his office. He didn't need a lathe, since no gas engine was involved. All he wanted was a basic airframe, a light electric motor, and one or two good batteries of the new type the government first used—rechargeable. All such stuff a chief engineer could take without anybody paying attention. Maybe he used radio control, or maybe he didn't need to. Perhaps he knew from dry runs at home with a prototype how far it would fly on a given charge. With fifty acres to crash in, he didn't have to be perfect. Probably he turned the model loose just when the real one roared over, just in case some sharp-eared busybody heard the faint whir of the props. It was such a good plan," Middlebie said, his enthusiasm growing, "that it ought to have succeeded."

"Who says it didn't? Even if you're right, there's nothing for the D.A. to take hold of. And I'm beginning to worry about you, Professor," the sergeant added gravely. "Lately you seem more on the side of the criminal than the law—emotionally, I mean."

"I'm on the side of imagination and ingenuity," Middlebie retorted, his voice chilly. "As for evidence, search that field. If the plane crashed there, you may find some traces. Dig until you can at least get a warrant, then maybe something will turn up at Brenner's house. Perhaps he was overconfident enough to save the prototype or some of the material he made it from. And run a bluff—you've done it before. Let him know you're on to him, and maybe he'll break."

"Naturally I'll do all that," Black said with dignity, and Middlebie grinned at him until he had to smile back.

"Mycroft couldn't do leg work, and neither can I," the old man said. "Don't think I like lying here; I'd rather be out at the bay watching the avocets."

"You'll be back there by the time I get my case against Brenner," Black assured him. And that's the way it was.

To Barbecue a White Elephant

Twice in a matter of days, Ulysses Price Middlebie, retired Professor of the History and Philosophy of Science, and now an unofficial crime consultant to his erstwhile pupil, Detective Sergeant Black, had performed like a Mycroft Holmes. Immobilized, by a badly sprained ankle, which he had sustained while climbing a steep bluff to photograph some nestling ravens, the vigorous old man had to operate on brain power alone, with Black as a willing and capable researcher. Like Sherlock's brother, the professor studied data brought to him by the sergeant, and offered suitable hypotheses to be tested against all the evidence. It was armchair detection of the most classical sort, and it compensated Middlebie for his forced inactivity, which he loathed.

He considered himself lucky in having two good cases brought to his attention in so short a time, and didn't expect another. He forgot— or didn't believe—the old superstition about things happening in threes.

So when Black called on the old man again, Middlebie assumed the visit was social, only to be delighted that it was not.

"No murder this time," Black grinned. "That makes it less interesting, I suppose."

"Not at all," the professor said, a little stiffly. "One can apply logic and reason just as effectively, and with the same intellectual satisfaction, to a problem of any type. A puzzling theft of fifty cents offers the same challenge as one of fifty million dollars."

"That's not the way the Department reacts," the sergeant said in a rueful voice. "The pressure goes up in proportion to the money value or the seriousness of the crime. If it's X for a liquor store robbery of eight hundred dollars, it's a million X—or X to the millionth—for the murder of a child."

"Is this case either?"

"No. It's a matter of arson. Nobody hurt. Just $100,000 insurance about to be collected, I'm afraid, and fraudulently."

"Isn't that a problem for the insurance company rather than the police?"

"Yes, but we usually work together. After all, our goal is the same: keep the law; nail the criminal."

"And what keeps you from—ah—nailing this one?"

"It's a question of method—time, actually. My arson experts don't think I can get a case."

The grey eyes lit up.

"What's the precise difficulty?" Middlebie demanded, shifting his bandaged ankle to a better position on the hassock.

"As I said—time. Here's a man gone for two months, stays in Mexico City, thousands of miles from his house. The place is locked up tight, and watched by a security company to boot; yet after six weeks a fire of unknown origin levels the building. The point is, nobody in the arson field admits there's any such thing as a six-week fuse. The fattest candle won't burn that long, and the other basic method, acid eating through a metal plate, is also out. The metal would have to be very thick; the acid would probably lose its bite before going through; and the arsonist would have to make a trial first—to time it—which would take a preliminary six weeks before he'd be ready for the real thing."

Middlebie was silent for a moment, his eyes clouded with thought.

"I'm inclined to agree," he said finally. "Six weeks of acid-eating seems very improbable. A really thick plate of that type might get such a coating of oxide and corrosion that the acid would stop working after a couple of weeks at most. As for a candle, I'd have to do some lab work but I believe that, beyond a certain size, the wick would have to be impossibly thick, or the candle itself many yards high and thin. Otherwise, the wick would burn down, leaving a hollow in a fat mass of wax, and so last only a couple of weeks, at best."

"That's about what my lab men say."

"Then why are you fighting them? What makes you sure it's arson?"

"I'll tell you, and you can check my reasoning. The house is a real white elephant, built in 1876. Taxes are high; income, nil. The owner can't sell it, can't maintain it; in fact, after he inherits the place—two years ago—he uses up a good part of the rest of his inheritance on minimum caretaking. The guy can't even abandon it. If the house isn't kept in the family, he forfeits the annuity and other benefits.

"Okay, he's in a box, so he does what most people—crooks, anyhow—do in that case. He insures the place for a fortune, fixes himself a good alibi, and burns it down."

"If so," the professor asked, "why couldn't he have hired somebody? He didn't have to be personally involved in setting the fire."

"The house was locked up tight, and every window has thick iron bars. You should see those doors—like a fortress. But that isn't all. As part of his alibi—at least, that's the way I see it—he hires a firm that specializes in guarding estates when the owners are away for long periods. They check it every day, and insist that every door was locked tight, and no bars tampered with."

"Then it comes to this," Middlebie said slowly. "All the evidence points to arson, but the time-lapse makes that a problem."

"Right."

"One thing. Why would any insurance company offer $100,000 coverage on a white elephant?"

"They like the premiums, which aren't small on that kind of deal, naturally. For another, the idea's got around—I'll bet the owner helped spread it—that the place might be leased and run by the state as a kind of historical monument. Then too, the way land values go up these days as cities expand, in ten years the place may be worth more than $100,000 just for the acreage. But the owner doesn't want to wait, I suppose, or can't afford to. It seems pretty clear that nobody went into the place while he was away, yet a fire starts inside and burns the guts out before anybody sends in an alarm. By the time the Fire Department trucks get up that rough county road, it was goodbye white elephant!"

"And hello to one hundred thousand dollars."

"Exactly. Unless you can figure out just how we were foxed. It wasn't any routine method that the pros use, I'll guarantee that. The arsonist came up with a really clever trick to get a blaze going deep inside a locked and guarded house."

"Perhaps. What do you know about him?"

"Old family, main heir, middle-aged playboy. Must have had his tongue out to inherit for years, but his mother lived to be ninety-three. She stuck him with keeping the house."

"Was she mentally competent?" Middlebie demanded. "If not, he could more easily break the will than take a chance on arson."

"She was eccentric, obviously, but not crazy. At ninety she wrote and sold an article about the old days in Vermont, and that makes her sane in my book. If she'd written some modern music for tin cans kicked by hobnails, her son might've had a case!"

"All right," the professor said. "Let's assume he did it. What's the house like, and where did the fire start, or do they know?"

"They know. It started upstairs, in one of the master bedrooms. There are nine bedrooms, each with a huge bathroom still equipped with the latest 1880 plumbing. The tubs are big enough for a whole modern family to bathe en masse; and the mirrors would blind anybody who didn't freshen up in sunglasses."

"How did it spread out of control so fast?"

"Here we're only guessing," the sergeant admitted. "The house is so big and solid that a lot of the interior was in flames before anything was noticed outside. When the gardener—who is no towering intellect—finally realized what was happening, he still had to get to a phone, and that's half a mile away. Everything was going for the arsonist. In addition, I suspect he spread plenty of newspapers and oily rags around. Not enough to leave obvious traces, but the right amount to keep the fire moving."

"Well," Middlebie said, "I'm willing to be Mycroft again, but this time there's even less to work with. You have a motive, certainly, and a good suspect, but nothing really of evidential value."

"Don't I know it," Black groaned. "The insurance company is ready to quit."

"I'll do what I can," the professor said. "I like the challenge of a six-week fuse. Suppose you get me all the data on the house and the man. What's his name, by the way?"

"Francis Raymond, IV, no less."

"Well, get me a good run-down on Mr. Raymond. For example, does he have any technical training, the sort that might suggest a really complex and sophisticated gadget?"

"I can answer that right now. He never took anything but courses in sociology, sandbox, and finger-painting, and he flunked most of those. He did very well on Advanced Blondes."

"Then I'll assume," the professor said, lips twitching in a brief smile, "that he dreamed up something basically simple, but ingenious. Maybe he should have been pushed into more demanding subjects—he might have made a good, imaginative scientist."

"There are no more demanding subjects than blondes," Black assured him. "Why do you think he needed that insurance money?"

"On your way," Middlebie said, ignoring the remark, "but get me a beer from the refrigerator before you leave."

Black did so, and strode out. He hated to see bourbon, beer, and brown sugar combined in one drink. Maybe it fired up the professor's unique brain, but it would have disintegrated the detective's stomach.

The next evening, Black brought over a great mass of papers, and for the following week Middlebie dutifully ploughed through the stack. Finally, after some days of this, he invited the young detective over for a discussion.

"I've gone through all the material you found," he said, "but really only one thing tends to implicate Raymond directly—although indirectly, to be accurate about it."

Black leaned forward eagerly. "Which is?"

"His going away for a long period was well publicized. More than that, he undertook the guarding of a house that he hated and would have been happy to see destroyed—by lightning, earthquake, fire, or flood. He would presumably have welcomed any vandalism that made the building a total loss, yet he hires an expensive private agency to watch it. The only reason, it would seem, is to give himself an alibi made up of distance and a concern for his property."

"That's what bothered me. He rigged something, and went far away while it did the dirty work. But how?"

"I don't know," the old man admitted frankly. "But now, like you, I feel that the psychology supports the idea of arson. So all we need now is the gimmick he used."

"That's all," Black said, his voice suspiciously meek.

Middlebie gave him a sharp, brief stare, and turned back to the heap of papers. The professor was studying utility bills, and gave a little dry cough of surprise.

"What've you got?" Black demanded.

"Very interesting." There was the hint of a Scots burr in Middlebie's speech. "No garden hose pipe or lawn sprinkler system, I see; nobody home to wash or drink. And yet in the first month—two weeks to go before the fire—he was billed for over eighty cubic feet of water. Now, why was water running at such a rate in an empty house?"

The detective looked at him blankly. "Sounds like a leaky washer. That's not uncommon, even in new places."

"That's what Raymond will say, I'm sure, but I doubt it. Oh, yes, I doubt it!"

"I don't see—"

"But I do, very plainly. There's one simple, obvious, and easily calibrated way to start a fire six weeks from now—or eight years, for that matter. You let water drip into a big bathtub—it would hold over a a hundred cubic feet, from the way you describe it—and measure the flow. Find out how long before the tub runs over; that's easy to do; just see how many buckets the thing will hold, and then see how long for a given trickle from the faucet to fill a bucket. It needn't be accurate to more than a few days, after all. He knew that after six to ten weeks he'd hear about a fire in the old homestead."

"How would an overflowing bathtub start a fire?"

"In a dozen ways. I could make the water drip into a glass of the right chemicals. I'd know, by trying it, just as he must have done, where that first trickle runs down the side of the tub when it's full. Assuming he didn't do that, there's a somewhat simpler approach. Let the overflow run into a glass on one end of a lever—a ruler, say—so that when the glass is partly full, it will spill acid into potassium chlorate or onto oily rags. A million ways, once you had the timer figured out."

Black gazed at him in a kind of awe.

"Damned if that isn't it; everything fits. He sets the thing up, goes away, presumably for many months, but knowing he'll be notified in weeks of the fire."

"He'll stick to the story of a bad washer—very convincing to any householder on a jury."

"Maybe. But I'll try to break him down. When they know we know, it seems to distract them—not always, but often."

"Good luck," Middlebie said. "When the case comes to trial—if it does—I hope to be at Oceanside, looking at some wood ibises."

The Puny Giant

"It was the footprint of a gigantic hound!" Professor Middlebie said dramatically.

Sergeant Black gaped at him, wondering if the old man's recent feats as an armchair detective in the tradition of Sherlock's fat, indolent brother, Mycroft, had suddenly affected his reasoning power.

"Hound?" he objected. "I didn't say anything about a dog at all—it was just a giant footprint."

"I know," Middlebie said, looking contrite. "It was an irresistible connection after all that Mycrofting. Sorry I interrupted; please go ahead."

As a former Professor of the History and Philosophy of Science, the old man was ideally trained to be an effective crime consultant. After all, to track down all the consequences of some unknown factor in a complicated laboratory experiment is not so different from identifying and outguessing a criminal, who leaves only subtle traces of his work.

"Well," Black said, "that part's a complete bust. We found the so-called giant or monster who'd scared a few people in the canyon; he's big enough—about six-three—and mighty spry, but the poor old guy's pushing seventy, and runs from anybody who comes close. We had a devil of a time catching him, and I felt as if I'd caged something meant to be free. Probably we'll give him some sanity tests, and let him go back to his cave. It's not clearly illegal to live that way, and he has no relatives to take care of him."

"And the footprint?"

"It certainly wasn't his. Oddly enough, for a big man, he has a small, narrow foot. Even funnier, the only size fourteen—which is actually what we're after—belongs to one of my own men, and he didn't kill the poor woman, believe me!"

"One print," Middlebie said thoughtfully. "Only one."

Black said, "It was the only really soft spot near the body. Still, I can't help feeling that the whole situation smacks of staging." He shook his head slowly. "But to stage this would call for supernatural help—ghosts, witches, or sorcerers."

"Let me summarize," the professor said. "See if I have the circumstances straight. You found the woman dead in the middle of a large lawn, well hidden by high hedges. She had been battered to death by a broken chunk of solid concrete, one that weighed over ninety pounds. And you're certain repeated blows were struck; it wasn't just dropped on her."

"That's right, and that's what stymies us. No, I'll retract that. Even if it had been just dropped on her, that's equally impossible. Nothing to drop it from; and to make such a wound—any of them, I mean— would call for a drop of eight or ten feet. Obviously, if the chunk were wielded like a blunt instrument, the killer would have to be a giant or a gorilla. You ever try battering with something weighing ninety pounds? It takes a mighty strong man to lift that much as high as his head—enough to maneuver it, that is. At first, we figured he may have dropped it on her several times, but the crime lab says there are scratches on her face and shoulders that indicate sweeping, pounding blows, fast-moving ones. Now what kind of athlete could swing that much weight so freely? Maybe a pro wrestler or All-American fullback could do it, but I'd have to be shown. And my only suspect now is a puny kid of sixteen."

Middlebie frowned. "Her son?"

"Adopted son. It could make some difference."

"Didn't they get along?"

"Pretty well, on the whole. He's a difficult boy, I'd say, partly because of his age—sixteen is murder for all kids. She was good to him, but not overtly affectionate, neighbors say. Apparently she adopted him as a baby, mainly to please her husband, since she couldn't have her own. Then, when he died while the boy was still an infant, she took care of him mostly from a sense of duty, it would seem."

"Was he much trouble?" Middlebie asked.

"No more than average, I suppose. But a young widow, who hadn't really wanted him to begin with—I don't know; who can figure these things? Actually, the boy's very bright, good in science, and even in art; dabbles in ceramics and such things, making vases and figurines."

"No other suspects, you say? No enemies? No motive at all?"

"I can't find any. She wasn't a popular type; kept to herself; was rather rigid morally. But in no way offensive enough to cause hatred. Her neighbors simply let her alone."

"Any money to inherit?"

"A few thousand dollars, life insurance, mostly. To her adopted son."

The professor's lean face was dark, his deep-socketed eyes brooding.

"I'd hate to think she was killed by her own son—even if only by adoption. The old Greeks had a point, you know. There is something abhorrent about that type of crime." He was silent for a moment, then said: "I still don't see just why you suspect him at all. He had so little to gain, a few thousand dollars. It's not as if they hated each other," he said softly.

"I know," Black admitted. "That's what gets me. But we've gone over the whole country looking for a giant who bashes people with ninety-pound concrete blocks, and there isn't any such. You can't be that big and ferocious without somebody spotting you. Except for that footprint—one lousy mark—there isn't a thing. Even if there were such a monster, how did he get to this corner of the community and pick this harmless woman sitting quietly in a chair in the middle of her lawn? She wasn't senile, only forty, and yet this hulking brute can walk up behind her with a boulder the size of a suitcase. It just doesn't make sense! Nobody heard her scream or call out. First anybody knows, the boy finds her body."

"All right," Middlebie said calmly. "You feel that the footprint may be phony. Let's assume that it is. That's the easy part. A boy handy with his fingers like this one could make a fake sole from wood or papier-mâché, stamp the muddy ground, and dispose of the gadget. That still leaves the concrete block, which only a giant could handle, and a motive, to tie in with the boy."

"There is a motive, of sorts," Black said reluctantly.

The professor gave him a sharp glance. "Took you long enough to say so."

"Because it isn't enough—and yet, people do kill each other over the most ridiculous things. A man battered an old friend to death just the other day because he thought the guy cheated him matching pennies. The amount involved was eighteen cents!"

"Was this a matter of money—the insurance, say?"

"Maybe." Black sucked in his cheeks. "These kids today! Here's this Julian—that's his name—bright, could be an engineer or physicist. Or an artist, maybe, if that's what he prefers. You'd think a boy like that wouldn't be as weird as the dropouts, the hot-rodders, the beats. And yet the only thing he and his stepmother quarreled about—and violently, if you believe the neighbors and the kid's friends—was his wanting a new car. He had his heart set on a red sports car, though he hadn't earned more than fifty dollars in his life. He wanted her to put out three thousand or so for this car. She told him the money would be a lot more useful for college. She was a cashier at a cafeteria, and sixty bucks a month on a sports car would have been plain silly. But he was wild to get it; nothing else seemed to matter."

"And you really think he killed this woman, this mother who took him in and cared for him, over an automobile?"

"I *don't* say that. I just can't help wondering. I have to check it out. I didn't say I liked the idea."

The professor said, "The first point I'd raise as a possible flaw in your reasoning is your assumption that the block did the killing. How do you know somebody—and even a puny boy could do this—didn't kill her with a club or hammer, and then smear the concrete with blood? That would clear up the matter of superhuman strength."

"It would," the detective replied, "and we thought of it. In fact, if you had asked me about that angle on the day of the murder, I'd have bet a month's salary it was done just so. But we have the new spectroscopic equipment that matches material beyond question. I don't have to tell you that when two spectrograms agree, what with hundreds of lines, there's less chance of error than with fingerprints. Well, fragments of dust, and the most minute particles of matter in her wounds and hair all match the outer surface of the concrete block. Nothing else struck her, and the block absolutely must have."

Middlebie said, "I congratulate you on your careful work and fine logic."

"Which I learned in your classes," Black said tactfully, and with complete accuracy.

The professor continued, "We agree that the block could not have been dropped from a plane or any structure. The repeated blows and the necessary height eliminate that possibility. Are there trees around? I'm thinking of a wire on which a pulley ... but I can't see a boy building a set-up like that, and giving the huge block repeated runs down it."

"No trees, anyhow," Black told him. "Not spaced that way, at least."

"Did you trace the block itself?"

"Yes and no."

"Meaning what?" Middlebie sounded irritated.

"Well, a few blocks from the house is a beach with hundreds of concrete blocks. They came years ago for use on the breakwater, and since then others have been dumped from leftover construction work and other things. This may have come from there. It would have had to come in a truck or car, of course, and we tried to trace that. Nobody saw any such stone delivered at or near the boy's place."

"If we go back to your original idea, that the whole thing was staged, then we're supposed to think a giant killed her. It follows that there must be some way a boy of sixteen could have done it, using a ninety-pound block like a single brick."

"I guess so." Black seemed gloomy. "I'd rather not believe he did it, but it's my job to find out, and a good cop has certain instincts ..."

"Very well, then. Maybe I'd better look at the block."

"It's just a hunk of concrete," the sergeant said listlessly. "But be my guest. We still have it in the crime lab. Come any time."

"I'll be down tomorrow morning," Middlebie said.

"What are you looking for?"

"I've no idea at all; not yet. I'll wait until I see the thing."

"Good," Black said. "Tomorrow morning, then."

When Professor Middlebie got to the Courthouse Building the next morning, Black was about to question the boy, Julian, again, and the old man had a sudden whim to sit in. In all his work with the sergeant so far, he had never even seen a suspect, except in photos. Besides, he was naturally sympathetic to the young, and especially those with talent.

Black was obviously surprised at his decision, but pleased.

"Now you can see how the other half lives," he jibed.

"I presume you use smaller rubber hoses on juveniles," the professor came right back, and the detective blinked.

An official of the Juvenile Court brought Julian to the Interrogation Room. He was a slight boy, with a variety of nervous mannerisms. His was clearly not the build to sling ninety-pound concrete blocks around, the old man thought. But, on the other hand, perhaps bright enough and imaginative enough to set a deceptive scene.

After some preliminary questions, Black made a more direct attack, obviously attempting to break the boy down.

"That car you wanted so much—the red sports car," he said casually, "I suppose you'll be buying it soon. Your mother managed to save most of your father's—stepfather's, I mean—insurance, didn't she?"

"Yes," Julian replied suspiciously. "There's enough for that."

"But she wanted to keep all she could for your college expenses."

"That's more than two years away. By then, I'd have a job."

Then Black threw his Sunday punch.

"I'm surprised that a boy as smart as you are didn't realize that the money can't be touched."

Julian gaped at him. "It's mine! The will says so; she told me. There's nobody else—no relatives."

"But you're a minor," the sergeant said gently. "The court will appoint a guardian. And I don't think any responsible adult will let you spend a third of your mother's estate on a sports car."

"But that's not right! It's my money. I'm no baby." His face had fallen in as if the bone structure had melted. "If I'd known that ..." he said, almost in a whisper.

"You killed her, didn't you?" Black asked, his voice casual.

It didn't work. The boy's frail body stiffened, and he glared defiance.

"Like hell I did! You saw that hunk of concrete." He gave a bitter laugh. "The kids call me a little creep. Can't you just see me swinging that block around?" His voice was full of self-pity. "That's why a guy needs a car. What good's her old 1957 model? The girls won't—" He broke off, biting his lips. "I'm not saying any more. I didn't do anything."

After that it was useless, so Black sent him back.

"Well?" he asked Middlebie.

"I'm not a psychologist," the old man said. "But judging from his despair over not getting the money—and the car—"

"Exactly. But how did he do it? If he did it."

"Let me examine that concrete block. I have one idea, at least, but it's pretty wild. It just might work."

In the laboratory, Black showed him the murder weapon. It was basically cubical in shape, but with rough, irregular edges, and seemed to have been broken off at some time from a larger piece.

"Probably came from some demolished old building foundation," the detective said.

Middlebie ran his fingers over the rough mass, then rested a palm on the top. His eyes narrowed.

"It feels a bit warm!" he exclaimed. "Was the sun shining on it through the window?"

"Not in here," Black said. "Now that you mention it, the block was warm when we first brought it here. It had been out in the hot sun for hours. We didn't hear about the murder until she'd been dead almost half a day, you know. Julian was away, and nobody else came into the yard."

The professor felt the surface again.

"As simple as that!" he breathed.

"What're you talking about?" Black demanded.

"Have you got an electric drill here? Quarter inch, with a bit for concrete?"

"I suppose so. We're pretty well stocked with tools."

"Well, get it then."

A bit huffily, the detective obeyed. Middlebie plugged the drill into a handy outlet, and began to work on the concrete. The special bit dug into the coarse aggregate, making plenty of noise. After piercing to a depth of three inches, the old man pulled out the drill, and peered into the hole. Then he examined the material powdered by the bit. His long index finger deftly found and separated some tiny grains of yellowish matter.

"Wood," he said cryptically. "So that's it."

"Will you please tell me—!" Black demanded in exasperation.

"Under this outer shell," the professor said, "is a wooden box, and in that box, fresh concrete, only partially cured, still moist and warm from the chemical reactions of a new mix. Don't you see?"

"Damned if I do—unless—"

"The boy made a shell after doing some calculating on the volume needed to get a mass of around a hundred pounds, something definitely too big for a small lad to handle. Probably he saw those references to a giant in the canyon and thought he had a good scapegoat. So he moulds this shell, lets it harden for a week, and then uses it to batter his stepmother to death. Right after that, he fills the hollow shell with more concrete, I'd guess the ready-mix kind, and then—"

"What a jerk!" Black moaned. "I saw the garage with paint, putty, and a sack of the quick-mix stuff in plain sight. And it didn't get through my bonehead!"

"Mine wasn't much thinner," the old man said grimly. "That sixteen-year-old almost fooled two veterans like us." His eyes were sad. "What a waste of brains! And for a miserable gadget like a sports car."

"He'll break now," the sergeant said, his voice full of satisfaction. "He's bound to."

The next day, when Black talked to Middlebie, the detective was understandably bitter.

"Do you know what bothered him most?" he asked ironically. "He was afraid that when he got out, at twenty-one, he might have trouble getting a new driving license."

The Symmetrical Murder

"You're like the White Queen—or was it the Duchess?—asking me to believe the impossible, just by trying."

"I'm not asking you to believe anything," Sergeant Black objected in turn, giving Professor Middlebie a rather sly glance, and avoiding a direct meeting of eyes.

The old man, formerly a teacher of the History and Philosophy of Science, and now, after retirement, a crime consultant in behalf of a one-time pupil, saw through the maneuver, and smiled.

"If you're trying to hook me," he said, "don't be so oblique; it isn't necessary. A really tricky puzzle is all you'll ever need, and this one seems to meet top requirements. Let's have the gist of it again."

"With pleasure," Black said. "It's stumped me, my staff, and a very bright insurance investigator." He opened his notebook, took a breath, and began.

"The victim was a Howard Davis Valind, a man of fifty-nine. By profession a cancer-quack, or mass murderer; wealthy, cynical, smart, and now very dead.

"He was staying at a seaside hotel; had been there for several weeks, even though it's the off season. He had an apartment on the second floor, with a balcony overlooking the ocean.

"Well, on a Monday afternoon, with a heavy fog blanketing the area, Valind came out, as usual, to throw some bread to the seagulls. It doesn't seem too bright of him; I don't know how he expected the birds to catch the hunks in midair with all that fog around, but nevertheless we found a bag of stale bread out there with him—with his body, that is. He was killed, about four, by an extremely powerful blow with something quite heavy—or, to be more precise—something moving with a lot of momentum and weight, or so heavy it didn't need much speed."

"What you're trying to say," Middlebie broke in rather impatiently, "is that either he was killed by something moderately heavy and fast-moving, or something massive but slower."

"Exactly," Black said, unabashed. "But which it was, we have no idea, and no shadow of a clue to help us decide. All right," he continued, "murder weapon unknown, but that's the least puzzling part of the affair. Valind was on the balcony, which is roofed against weather. He was roughly twenty feet above the ground, and his apartment door was locked and bolted. Yet he gets his skull smashed to flinders by somebody, who didn't leave a trace of himself or his bludgeon. That's what has us climbing the walls."

For a moment the professor was silent, then he said, "I can't visualize the balcony in relation to the hotel. Have a sketch or a photo?"

"Both," the sergeant said promptly, opening his briefcase. "Here they are." He put a glossy eight by ten print on Middlebie's desk, and beside it a scale drawing. Middlebie carefully studied them both. The hotel, as seen from a balloon directly overhead, was shaped like a "C" made up of three rectangles. The main body of the building was a three-story, box-like structure, from which two identical wings extended. Each wing held three apartments vertically, all with balconies. The building and two wings enclosed a kind of court, with its third side open to the sea. The balconies extended inside the "C", as well as along the part fronting on the water.

"Perfectly symmetrical," Middlebie said. "You noticed that, I suppose? Directly across the court from Valind's apartment is an identical one, with its inner balcony facing his."

"You bet we did," Black said fervently. "It's an ideal spot from which to shoot or throw something. But that cat won't jump an inch. If the occupant threw anything heavy, and crushed Valind's skull, what happened to it? When the maid found the body in the morning, there was no weapon—nothing heavy."

"How about something small and fast-moving? You said that might account for the injury."

"I didn't say 'small.' The whole side of his head was mashed in. Slow and heavy and big, or fast and big, but not very small. Nothing big enough to do the job could have been projected in any way we can think of. And if there were a catapult or anything that wild, we still have the question of what happened to the projectile."

"Well," the professor said slowly, "if the killer tied a line to it ..."

"A good point," Black said, his voice bitter. "Which leads me to our second impossibility. Because of tide conditions, the sand in the court, and down to the water, was smooth between noon and the next morning. There wasn't a suspicious mark on it. If any rock or club heavy enough to do the killing had been hauled back across the court from one balcony to its mirror image, there would have had to be marks in the loose sand. Well, nothing was found except the manager's prints, and those of a janitor; both were carefully checked out. Besides, there was no way to strike Valind such a blow from down there."

"What about the roof?"

"Same thing. No dice. Valind was hit on the side of the head, and anyhow, all balconies are covered. The apartment over him has been vacant for several days, and is useless as a base for that kind of blow."

"But surely an agile man could climb from that apartment's balcony down to Valind's," the professor pointed out.

"He could, but nobody did. The killer would have had to go past a desk clerk while carrying the weapon. Then he would have to get through the locked door of the upper apartment. Finally, and this clinches it, the place had newly varnished floors, which nobody had stepped on. And if you're wondering about the one below Valind's, that belongs to the manager, a Mr. D'Agostino, and his wife was there all day."

Middlebie was frowning, and Black had a sudden unhappy feeling that sooner or later a case would come along that was obscure enough to stop even a man of the professor's ability in logic and imagination. And maybe this was the one.

The old man picked up the scale drawing again. "The two balconies are thirty feet apart—measured across the court ..." he said to nobody in particular. "Sand unmarked. No access to Valind's balcony from his apartment or the ones above and below. Went out to feed seagulls; thick fog … hm." He looked at Black. "Was that a fixed habit, something that happened on schedule?"

"Right. You've put your finger on a significant point. Whoever planned this might very well have taken that into account. He'd know that Valind would step out on his balcony around four to feed the gulls. Odd," the sergeant added darkly, "how these swine who prey on the most pitifully helpless humans, the fatally ill, often turn out to be such great animal lovers."

"Yes," Middlebie said absently. He picked up the photo again, and scrutinized the two balconies. They faced each other across the court, and each extended around the corner of its wing to offer an ocean view as well. Below, opposite the ocean side of the "C" shaped court, was the main entrance of the hotel, a high, arched doorway; well above it was a window opening on the big staircase, and just below that a heavy bracket apparently set there to hold a flag on suitable occasions. None of these items of information seemed to help the old man very much. He dropped the picture back on the desk, and slowly shook his head.

"My mind's a total blank," he said frankly. "I can't imagine how it was done. From what you say, nothing could have been thrown from any of the three obvious vantage points: the apartments above and below, and the balcony opposite. Further, if anything had been projected to Valind's balcony, what could have spirited it away afterwards? And the unmarked sand makes things even more hopeless." He paused. "What about motive? Any clues there?"

"With a guy like this," Black said in a dry voice, "motive's no problem. Thanks to Valind, a lot of people died of cancer that might have lived. They died broke, full of quack remedies like molasses and aspirin at ten dollars a bottle; or a salve made of vaseline, zinc, cocoa butter, and salt, at a dollar a dab."

"Manager below," Middlebie muttered. "Nobody over. Who was across the day of the killing?"

"A man named Franklin—Crosby Franklin. He was our prime suspect."

"Why?"

"His sister had a cancer, a skin thing that a minor operation might've cured easily. Instead, she went to Valind. His salve spread the stuff, so that she lost half her face; not even an expensive plastic job, paid for by brother Crosby, could salvage her looks. She killed herself a few months later."

The professor's lips were narrow and tight.

"Why the devil didn't she go to a regular M.D.?" he demanded.

"She did, poor woman. Maybe he was a bit tactless, but anyhow the mention of cancer and operation simply scared her to death. Her brother was away in another state; she got panicky and took a stupid friend's advice about seeing the miracle man—no knife ever used!—Valind."

"Pity," Middlebie said. "When will this kind of thing be stopped for good?" He sighed. Then his eyes lit up. "At least, that narrows the field. I think we should assume that Franklin might have done the killing. Now, could he operate from his balcony? That's the vital point. And if so, how? I just don't see it."

Once more he scrutinized picture and diagram. His shaggy brows went down over the deep-set eyes.

"Franklin knew about the fog and the gull feeding. He was in that apartment for a few days, I presume?"

"Yes, he came not long after Valind; may have followed him, in fact. All he'd have to do is watch the man's behavior. Valind was running scared, whether of Franklin or somebody else, we don't know. No record of any threats by Franklin, but he's the quiet type that acts, I suspect. Valind never went on the beach alone; kept his place well locked. But he felt safe on the balcony, although the manager did tell me Valind would watch anybody around or across. If he spotted a kid with a .22 rifle on the beach, he'd scoot off the balcony. That's how spooked he was. Bad conscience, I suppose. Actually, if Franklin's our man, he had no plan to shoot Valind and pay the penalty; he intended to kill the guy clean, and not be caught or even leave a clue. That's how it's worked out, anyway."

"The body was found by the maid next morning."

"Yes."

"The only prints on the sand were the manager's and a janitor's?"

"Right again."

"What was the manager doing out there?" Middlebie asked.

"Nothing much; I guess he usually goes out in the morning to see the condition of the beach, and to chase off any trespassers. He didn't find any, but he was certainly mad about the flag."

"Flag? What flag?" The professor's voice was sharp.

Black grinned.

"Monday was Columbus Day—did you know that? Well, D'Agostino is Italian, and had a big flag flying over the entrance. The janitor or somebody should have taken it down at sunset, around five-thirty this time of year. But he goofed, and it was out all night in the damp and fog. So D'Agostino was spitting mad. You'd think Columbus was his son, and the American Flag alive."

"It shouldn't be left out that way," the old man said simply. "Aside from the question of hyper-patriotism, there's a matter of good taste and custom." He picked up the photograph again. Then he took a large magnifying glass from a desk drawer and studied the bracket over the entrance to the hotel. Quickly, he turned his attention to the scale drawing.

"Height of bracket," he murmured, "thirty feet, or ten feet higher than the balconies." He pulled a slide rule from a pigeonhole, and made some lightning calculations. "With an eighteen-foot rope—yes, it checks out. Very neat—very neat, indeed. It must have been done that way."

"What?" Black cried. "You lost me about nine decimal places back!"

"Notice that the bracket holds the flagstaff almost horizontally," the old man said, ignoring the detective's plea. "That's important."

"Is it?" Black gulped. "Mind telling me why?"

Middlebie put down the slide rule, and pencil in hand, made a quick sketch.

"This is very rough and symbolic," the professor said, quite unnecessarily, "but the point is clear. All Franklin had to do was toss a double eighteen-foot rope fifteen feet out and up ten feet to loop over the horizontal flagstaff not far from the flag end. Anything heavy tied to his end of the rope at his balcony, level with his face, would, because of the obvious symmetry (I should have considered that symmetry at once!) when released, swing up to practically the same point on Valind's balcony. He must have got ready in the fog, knowing that his victim would step out and stand at the corner of the balcony opposite while feeding, or trying to feed, the seagulls. When he hears Valind out there, Franklin pulls the heavy object, perhaps a rock from the beach, taken to his room several nights earlier, up well past his own head, and then lets go. It's like a great pendulum in action. The rock swings in a perfect circular arc from Franklin's corner to Valind's, crushing in the side of his skull. Then, on the return swing, Franklin catches the rock—easy enough as it hesitates before beginning another cycle—unties it, slips the doubled rope off the staff, and no trace of the method is left. Unless, perhaps, you can find some mark on the wood, paint rubbed off, that sort of thing. He probably tossed the rock off the seaward side of his balcony into the surf. I suppose there are other rocks on the shore."

"A million," Black said. "And this one washed clean by now. Pounding saltwater would remove any blood or tissue in a few hours. But how could Franklin have counted on that flag? Without it, there was no fulcrum for the pendulum."

"Hard to say," Middlebie admitted. "Possibly D'Agostino talked about Columbus Day in advance, or maybe Franklin himself suggested that flying the flag would be in order. If I may presume to enter the mind of the man, I might infer that Franklin followed Valind to the hotel determined to kill him at any cost. Maybe his first impulse was to shoot him from the balcony opposite, or even to crash the man's room, and murder him there, taking the consequences afterwards. But then he saw the bracket, and noted the symmetry of the two wings, each with matching balconies, and it occurred to him that it might just be possible to get Valind, and escape unsuspected, or unconvicted. After that, he would work out details, check the thickness of the flagstaff, and make use of Columbus Day. Failing that, there would be other ways to get the manager to display a flag. I'm more puzzled," the old man said, "by the part played in the killing by fog. It would normally come in by late afternoon this time of the year, but Franklin couldn't count on it absolutely. In that case, he must have been prepared to let his victim see the rope; maybe he hoped Valind would consider it part of the flag-raising equipment, ignore it, and with his back turned, feeding seagulls, could still be killed by a quick release of the rock pendulum."

"You may be right—and probably are," Black said. He hesitated, then, his face showing doubt. "But there's one thing that isn't too convincing. You calculated he'd need a double eighteen-foot rope, say forty feet. All right, he holds one end, and flips the other over the staff, fifteen feet out and ten up. How does he get the free end back to his balcony then, so he can complete the pendulum set-up and tie on the rock?"

Middlebie's face was suddenly blank; he flushed.

"Hmm," he said. "It wouldn't be too easy, at that. The loose end, with a small weight, might swing back, but I doubt it. And you don't find fifteen-foot sticks in hotel rooms very often."

"I've got it!" Black cried then. "Right under my nose." He grinned at the professor. "Franklin did a lot of fishing while stalking Valind. He had several surf rods in his room. Wouldn't that explain it?"

"It certainly should," Middlebie said. "A surf-fishing pole could be from nine to twelve feet long, easily. With one of those, a few more feet of line, with hooks, to whip around the dangling rope, and he'd have no problem bringing the other end back to his balcony. Score one for you," he added.

"Well, it all adds up," the sergeant said, "but I don't see how much of it will stand up in court. Too hypothetical and tricky."

"That's your baby," the old man said, his face wooden.

Black gave him a keen glance. "You don't really want Franklin nailed, do you?"

"Guilty," Middlebie said, without embarrassment. "I tried to solve the puzzle; that's purely intellectual pleasure. Morally, I may be way off base, but I hate cancer quacks. I did what I could. I have no competence to build up a court case for the D.A. If he can convict Franklin, he'll undoubtedly do so, and you'll help. But if you both fail, that won't be my fault, and I don't intend to cry about it."

You sophistic old devil! the sergeant exclaimed, but silently. Aloud he said merely, "You're right, of course. I'll try for some direct evidence, but the prognosis is bad."

"That's a pity," Middlebie responded, without a trace of regret.

Fire for Peace

"Fire and fanaticism are a bad combination." Ulysses Price Middlebie spoke with unusual gravity, which the situation seemed to warrant.

"It's even worse than that," Sergeant Black said. "The place is full of inflammable chemicals—and explosives, too."

"Just what are they making?"

"I couldn't say—officially. Nobody's supposed to know. But it's the old story; every person in the county has it figured out. Some joker always talks. It's nerve gas and some other hush-hush chemical warfare stuff. So you can imagine how wild they are about these incendiaries popping up all over the place, in spite of the most careful precautions."

Middlebie, recently retired as Professor of the History and Philosophy of Science, and now a crime consultant, fixed his grey eyes on the detective, and said: "But surely this is a federal matter. Where's the F.B.I.?"

"Everywhere!" was the bitter retort. "Oh, they're polite enough, and talk about 'cooperating' with the local law enforcement agencies; but some of them are so blasted patronizing, I expect to be patted on the head. Call it jealousy, but I'd like to crack this case before they do—and you're my secret weapon!"

The professor was silent for a moment, as if taking stock. There was a series of Audubon-sponsored bird trips to the Bay, for which he would be responsible. Not to mention his talk to the High School Science Club on the mathematics of space flight. He frowned.

"How long has the F.B.I. been on the case?" he demanded.

"Several weeks now."

"Any results?"

"Not that I can see," Black said dryly. "They checked the security measures, decided it must be an inside job, and urged the brass to institute a complete lie-detector program—test every soul working there. Well, that was done, and nothing came of it. After all, the employees have top clearances for mental stability and such things. I could have told them you won't find many pacifist diehards turning out deadly gasses. So they're back where they started—and even more baffled, if you ask me."

"That's the big group of buildings north of the airport?"

"Right. Should be a cinch to guard. Mostly open country, with no other buildings around for several hundred yards in each direction. Big wire fence; complete change of clothes coming and going; airtight search—it all came up blank. Yet the fires keep breaking out."

Black saw the grey eyes glisten, and felt a thrill of satisfaction. He had the old boy hooked. Nobody was more of a sucker for a really tricky puzzle. Once he knew that the obvious solutions didn't apply, and that other experts were stumped, Middlebie simply had to try his hand.

"Well," he said, seemingly casual, but with that glint in his eyes to betray him. "There's no harm in listening to a few details. Lay it out for me as concisely as you can. But don't overdo the condensation."

"You bet!" Black replied, making no effort to hide his satisfaction. "First came the letters. The federal boys kept those, but here are photos." He placed six eight by ten glossy prints on Middlebie's desk. "As you see, printed in pencil on a cheap writing pad—the safest way. No messing with cut-out letters from magazines; nothing too smart. Probably disguised the block-printing, even though it's never much of a clue."

"Hold up a minute, while I read these," the professor said.

The notes were all quite similar, each taking the form of an ultimatum. A typical one read: "I hear that last fire almost got away from you. Next time it will be several at once. Be reasonable and close down the plant. Otherwise it will burn, and people may be killed or hurt. Your guards are useless against me." It was signed, "Committee of One, for Peace."

"Seems literate enough," Middlebie said thoughtfully. "Not like some of the wild-eyed brethren with new religious revelations."

"Literate, intelligent, technically trained—and damned effective!" Black said in a grim voice.

"Hm. You can continue now," the professor said, a bit pompously.

"Well, one of the incendiaries was a dud, and they found it. All I can show you is a photo; the F.B.I. sent the thing itself to their crime lab in Washington. But I did get to examine it. They tell me it's very similar to the kind used in World War II. Tiny; weighs almost nothing; but very powerful; goes off with a spurt of flame that lasts for almost a minute, and can set fire to nearly anything that will burn."

Middlebie was studying the photograph, first with the naked eye, then with a good lens.

"Is that a bit of string tied to it?" he demanded.

"Yes; and that's about the only clue we have as to how the bombs are delivered. Not that it helps much."

"Whirled slingshot fashion, to fall over the fence?"

"Impossible. The grounds are patrolled night and day—with dogs, too."

"Dropped from a plane?"

"Again, no. Forbidden area; nobody flies over unless he wants the C.A.A. and the Army Air Force after him. In fact, he'll be lucky if they don't send a missile up his tail."

"How many fires so far?"

"Twelve. The first four were singles: one each week, with a letter the day after, demanding closing of the plant. When the warning was ignored, the next fire in seven days. Talk about thumbing his nose at the precautions."

Middlebie studied the photo again.

"Looks home made."

"It is. Just a bit of aluminum tubing, acid, and chemicals. The kind anybody with know-how can buy from those places that advertise in the mechanics magazines. This bird may have done some demolition work in Korea or Germany. One dud out of thirteen isn't so amateurish. But it's the delivery that really shows genius."

"Where's the nearest cover? That is, where could a man hide near the plant, and not be seen by the guards?"

Black reflected for a moment.

"Well, there are brushy hills a few hundred yards away. But nothing much any closer."

"And at night?"

"Plenty of floodlights. A man might be able to get within, oh, I don't know—two hundred yards of the plant."

"I wonder," the professor said, half to himself, "if the bombs could be shot or projected from that distance."

"Impossible," Black said glumly. "I held one. It's too light; like trying to throw a packet of paper matches, for example. Even with something heavier—say, a pack of cigarettes—you just couldn't get such a range."

"It could be tied to something heavy; hence the string."

Black stiffened.

"That could be it!" he exclaimed. "The heavy part might've burned up; that's why we never found any."

"How about with the dud?"

"Maybe we missed it, not knowing what to look for."

"That's possible," Middlebie agreed. "In any case, all I can suggest for now is that you look for something heavy that might have been shot or thrown over the fence. Ask around, in case it has already been found and disposed of as casual trash. Then give me a ring—or another visit. Meanwhile, I'll think the problem over. Oh yes; leave the photos, if you can."

Black hesitated.

"The feds wouldn't like it," he said; "but t'hell with that. I can trust you, or might as well give up my badge. Thanks a lot; I sure hope you hit the jackpot on that heavy-object bit." He shook the professor's hand, and left.

When the detective had gone, Middlebie went over the facts again; it was always easier to think clearly when alone; brainstorming just wasn't his dish. Almost at once he spotted the fallacy in his own theory. Obviously, if the fanatic wanted to toss incendiaries from a distance, either with a catapult or some kind of air-gun, it would be to his advantage to make them heavy enough for a good, long flight. No point in miniaturizing them, and then having to tie something weighty to each bomb in order to project it over the fence onto the plant itself. No, that idea was out. Which left what?

The professor shook his head. Alongside the set of pictures was a sheaf of typewritten papers—undoubtedly Black's detailed report of the case. It would be worth scrutinizing, but first a patent stimulator.

In a large glass he poured an ounce of bourbon, added a heaping spoonful of brown sugar, and filled it to the top with bock beer. His friends called this—with shudders—Middlebie's Bullfrog Gin: Drink a little; hop a little; and croak. He sipped the horrible stuff with relish, and read the detective's report. Certainly Black had learned lucidity and logic in the professor's class, five years earlier; Middlebie was pleased with the write-up.

There was one point, in particular, that still supported his theory of shooting the bombs over the fence. All the incendiaries had been found outside the buildings. Some on the roofs; but most in odd, dark corners of the structures; although a few had turned up in the grass only inches from a wall.

Middlebie examined the photo of the dud again. That string was intriguing; it didn't look strong enough to have held anything heavy tight against the bomb. It was all very puzzling. He studied the ragged end: cut or just snapped? It looked more like the latter—rough threads in a tangle.

The professor was tantalized by a memory, something just beyond the edge of his conscious mind. A pencil-shaped little bomb; a bit of string—surely they meant something familiar; something he'd read about a few years ago, and with interest, even wonder. Then, like a flashbulb, the light came. Excited, Middlebie pulled a county map from a desk drawer, and checked the western area. What he found there made him grin boyishly; the pieces were fitting together. But nobody knew better than he that the real test was the Baconian one of observation.

When Black phoned the next morning, he was annoyed to find the professor out. He couldn't know that Middlebie had taken a position, before dawn, on a bushy hill near the plant, and well hidden by the undergrowth, was stretched out with his 7 x 50 binoculars handy.

He lay there for almost six hours, alleviating the monotony by watching the numerous flocks of birds, and identifying them with the casual expertise of the ornithologist. A tremendous dividend, quite apart from the case, resulted; for he saw his first Bendire's thrasher, one of the rarest birds in this state. He was so excited he almost gave himself away to a possible enemy, but cooled off in time.

That evening, when the impatient sergeant finally found him at home, Middlebie was still more elated over the bird—after all, he was sixty-seven, and had never seen one until now—than his breaking of the case.

But as Black began to breathe harder, the professor took pity on him, and abandoned ornithology for criminology.

"So you want to scoop the F.B.I.?" he asked blandly. "Well, maybe I can tell you how to do it." He took the county map, opened it, and pointed with a lean finger. "Right here is Dutchman's Cave—ever hear of it?"

The detective looked bewildered.

"Vaguely."

"If you—what's that phrase?—stakeout the place for a day or two—and only by day—you should get your man."

Black gaped at him.

"Get my man? Who? Who am I looking for? How'll I know him?"

"Watch for a man—or a woman—who's catching bats in the cave."

Black stared at him speechlessly.

"Bats? Did you say bats?"

"Exactly. Free-tail bats. There are thousands in the cave."

Black gave up.

"Why would he be catching bats, for God's sake?"

"During the war," Middlebie explained patiently, "there was a plan to set Japanese houses—all wood and paper—on fire by releasing hundreds of free-tail bats from a plane. They had tiny incendiaries tied to their bodies. Now by day they are very anxious to get away from the light, and so fly to all the dark corners of buildings. Then they gnaw the string in two in order to get rid of the annoying load. That distributes bombs all over the place, and where nobody would think of looking, or even be able to reach.

"The scheme was actually tested on a wooden city built for the purpose, and it really worked—a little while after the bats were dropped, the whole place went up in smoke.

"And that's why these bombs at the plant appeared where they did. Our man just took up a spot a few hundred yards away—beyond the patrols—and turned his captive bats loose. I saw some flying in this morning, just before noon; I could even see the bombs. Bet they had about six fires today—right?"

"Five," Black muttered.

"One didn't go there, probably. But it is the only place high enough to attract them; all open fields, as you know."

"But with everybody watching—in broad daylight—!"

"He was out of sight, over the hill, I would guess. And hundreds of birds fly around the area, landing in and around the plant. How many people could spot a few flittering bats among all those birds? The swallows, for example, are quite similar in flight.

"You know," he added gravely, "I can almost sympathize with our fanatic friend. To add chemical horror to atomic destruction is pretty dreadful. They say non-resistance in the Christian tradition can't work, but certainly arms races haven't solved anything, ever. And the pacifist way has never so far even been tried; it can't do much worse, on the record." He sighed. "Well, I don't know the answer, yet I've seen to it that our disturbed friend will end up either in jail or the psycho ward. But you have no doubts, Black, eh—so go get him!"

"I do see your point," the sergeant said a bit stiffly, "but burning down the plant isn't so pacifistic, either!"

"I accept that," Middlebie said in a somber voice. "But then I've always preferred birds to people, and don't take human problems seriously. What a nice world this would be if the birds had it to themselves!"

Checklist of Sources

Note: The checklist below gives the original publication source for each of the stories included in this collection.

"These Daisies Told"
Alfred Hitchcock's Mystery Magazine, December 1962

"The Unguarded Path"
Mike Shayne Mystery Magazine, January 1963

"The Missing Bow"
Alfred Hitchcock's Mystery Magazine, November 1963

"Small, Round Man From Texas"
This Week (a Sunday magazine supplement to *The Los Angeles Times, The Salt Lake Tribune* and *The Cincinnati Enquirer*), February 16th, 1964

"Blood Will Tell"
Alfred Hitchcock's Mystery Magazine, February 1964

"Coffee Break"
Alfred Hitchcock's Mystery Magazine, July 1964

"A Model Crime"
Alfred Hitchcock's Mystery Magazine, August 1964

"To Barbecue a White Elephant"
Alfred Hitchcock's Mystery Magazine, October 1964

"The Puny Giant"
Alfred Hitchcock's Mystery Magazine, November 1964

"The Symmetrical Murder"
Alfred Hitchcock's Mystery Magazine, December 1964

"Fire for Peace"
Ed McBain's 87th Precinct Mystery Magazine, May 1975

About the Author

Arthur Porges was born in Chicago, Illinois on August 20, 1915. One of four brothers, he was educated at Roosevelt High School and Senn High School before enrolling at The Lewis Institute where he achieved a Bachelor of Science Degree in Mathematics. After the successful completion of his postgraduate studies, through which he attained Masters Degrees in Mathematics and Engineering from the Illinois Institute of Technology, Porges enlisted in the U.S. Army in 1942. During the Second World War he served as an artillery instructor, teaching algebra and trigonometry to field personnel. He was stationed at various military installations including Camp White in Oregon, Fort Sill, Oklahoma, Camp Roberts, California and at Barnes Hospital in Vancouver, Washington. After the war Porges returned to Illinois and taught mathematics at the Western Military Academy, going on to serve as an assistant professor at De Paul University. Having taught at Occidental College in Los Angeles for a brief stint in the late forties, Porges made a permanent move to California in 1951 and spent several years as a mathematics teacher at Los Angeles City College. During this period he wrote and sold short stories as a sideline. In 1957, Porges retired from teaching to write full-time. He went on to publish hundreds of short stories in numerous magazines and newspapers. Many of his stories appeared in *Alfred Hitchcock's Mystery Magazine*, *Ellery Queen's Mystery Magazine*, *Amazing Stories* and *The Magazine of Fantasy and Science Fiction*. His fiction spanned several genres, with tales ranging from science fiction and fantasy to horror, mysteries, and so on. At his most prolific his work was appearing in three or four periodicals in one month alone. Among his best-known stories are "The Ruum," "The Rats," "No Killer Has Wings," "The Mirror" and "The Rescuer." Twelve previous book collections of his short stories have been published: *Three Porges Parodies and a Pastiche* (1988), *The Mirror and Other Strange Reflections* (2002), *Eight Problems in Space: The Ensign De Ruyter Stories* (2008), *The Adventures of Stately Homes and Sherman Horn*

(2008), *The Calabash of Coral Island and Other Early Stories* (2008), *The Miracle of the Bread and Other Stories* (2008), *The Devil and Simon Flagg and Other Fantastic Tales* (2009), *The Curious Cases of Cyriack Skinner Grey* (2009), *The Ruum and Other Science Fiction Stories* (2010), *The Rescuer and Other Science Fiction* Stories (2014), *Unusual Plants of the Galaxy* (2014) and *No Killer Has Wings: The Casebook of Dr. Joel Hoffman* (2017). A keen birdwatcher and an avid reader, in later years Porges wrote many articles, essays and poems, most of which were published in the *Monterey Herald*. Several of his poems were collected in the book *Spring, 1836: Selected Poems* (2008). After spells in Laguna Beach and San Clemente, Porges moved north, eventually settling in Pacific Grove. He passed away, at the age of 90, in May 2006.